T0000218

"These are the most truthful stories about the film world and its suburbia I have ever read. Gavin Lambert knows and loves what he describes; he neither sneers nor sentimentalizes nor cries sour grapes."

—Christopher Isherwood

"Decades before it was fashionable, Gavin Lambert expertly wove characters of every sexual stripe into his lustrous tapestries of southern California life. His elegant, stripped-down prose caught the last gasp of old Hollywood in a way that has yet to be rivalled."

—Armistead Maupin

"Lambert's characters are narcissistic, selfish and manipulative. They're forever changing their addresses and phone numbers, but can't decide who they're running from . . . *The Goodby People* is his dark glory, melancholic, becalmed and effortlessly resonant."

—Christopher Fowler, *The Independent*

"One of the brightest, wittiest people I have ever known. I was never bored with him."

—Mart Crowley

THE GOODBY PEOPLE

GAVIN LAMBERT

McNally Editions

New York

McNally Editions
52 Prince St, New York 10012

Copyright © 1971 by Gavin Lambert
All rights reserved
Printed in China
Originally published in 1971 by Simon & Schuster, New York.
First McNally Editions paperback, 2022

ISBN: 978-1-946022-44-8
E-book: 978-1-946022-45-5

Designed by Jonathan Lippincott

1   3   5   7   9   10   8   6   4   2

To Natalie and Richard Gregson

THE GOODBY PEOPLE

PROLOGUE:
HER

On a late afternoon in late summer the air-pollution count is 0.37, and sunlight mists the headstone of a star who was born, then died young. Beyond the lines of markers a boulevard growls with traffic and a billboard on stilts announces Elvis Presley in Las Vegas. The distant Santa Monica mountains, blurred with heat and smoke, look as desolate as a photograph of the moon.

Between the graves, through the haze of gas and carbon, someone approaches. He's thin, pale, maybe twenty years old, with flowing Christlike hair and mirror sunglasses, so you can't see his eyes, only yourself reflected. White T-shirt, old Levis, bare feet. He hurries past the markers, carrying three apricot-colored roses that blush at the center and faint at the edges.

Without noticing me, he lays the roses on the star's grave. I step up behind him and say, "Excuse me." His whole body quivers, then goes tense, as if he expects to be arrested. I explain I've read in a gossip column about this person who comes every Saturday afternoon to lay three

3

roses on the grave of this star, and I waited for him last Saturday but he didn't show up.

He turns around and stares at me. His mouth twitches a little at the corners. "Oh! . . . I had the virus. And my throat ached. I felt just too terrible to go out. Even—" he indicates the grave—"for *her*." He puts a cigarette in his mouth. "I hope it doesn't seem wrong to you to smoke here, but I'm a completely addictive personality. You have no idea! Do you interpret my smoking in this place as a lack of respect?"

I tell him no. There's no reason to make a *thing* out of cemeteries. All these people under all these markers are just dead. If they were buried alive, it might be different.

"Yes. My mother was *her* housekeeper, you know. Just for a month."

An innocent. It never occurs to him to question my curiosity. He was alarmed for a moment, but he really *wants* to talk about what he's doing. A loner too. He talks to strangers because he has no friends.

"It didn't work out, *she* and my mother didn't get along, but . . ." He gives an excited gasp. "One day I came to the house to visit my mother and *she* was there! And I was introduced! And I brought her roses—you might say I was prepared for the event of her being there—just like the ones I bring her now. She *adored* the color! And although she wasn't hitting it off with my mother, and who shall blame her, she couldn't have been more—well, more *beautiful* to me. But then, she was—" a long sigh—"beautiful."

He pauses, waiting for me to agree with him. His mouth twitches slightly again. I tell him yes, she was very beautiful.

"She asked what I did and I told her nothing yet, but I thought maybe I'd learn to type and all that, so I might try and become a secretary. You know? To someone in show biz?"

The sun peers through a gap in the haze. His mirror-lenses catch it, making specks of light dance all over the graves.

"Do you know what she said? Can you guess? She *encouraged* me! She actually said, 'Well, if you do that, if you learn to type, you come back and see me.' I almost died." He blows out smoke. "And then *she* died. And I can't get her out of my mind."

He looks at the grave with the three roses. He runs his fingers across her name carved in stone.

"I've never known such kindness and sheer sweet thoughtfulness from a person like that—from *any* person —since the day I was born. She was so beautiful and so thoughtful. And then she died. And I can't get her out of my mind."

All this time there's been a growl of traffic outside the cemetery. Now I hear a slam of brakes, and it sounds like a sudden deranged cry.

"They say that people who are very beautiful never *belong!* They say they *can't love.* But I have proof these statements are completely untrue!"

BORN JULY 17, 1935.
DIED AUGUST 4, 1967.

"*She* loved. Even to a nobody she was full of love. You know why?" His voice rises, like the slam of brakes. "People like that, you just have to *understand* them. Reach out! Then they'll *stay* . . ." Below the mirror-sunglasses a single tear wobbles down each cheek. He wipes one of them away, smiling at the same time, and repeats like a phonograph needle stuck in a groove, "But then she died. And I can't get her out of my mind." He looks at the grave again and bends toward her name. "Got to be going now," he says, rather apologetic. "Goodby."

SUSAN ROSS

On a late afternoon a few days later, a butler who looks rented says, "Mrs. Ross thought you might like to wait on her beach."

It occurs to me that someone who's never met Susan, nor even heard of her, could guess from this the following: She is a woman who sends emissaries, she assumes you know she'll keep you waiting, she apologizes by trying to make the waiting enjoyable, and she would never abandon you to a public beach.

I follow the butler through the rented house, all concrete, glass, sectional couches, neutral wall-to-wall carpet, sliding screens and doors. By the time we reach the patio the light has begun to fade. The butler in his tuxedo is a silhouette against the ocean. He opens a final glass door and points a black arm toward a table topped by an umbrella, surrounded by chairs with cushions in bright Hawaiian flower patterns. On the table I notice a silver cigarette box, a silver vase of orange carnations, copies of *Vogue, Réalités,* the *National Geographic Magazine.* The surf breaks with an even thud.

The butler asks what I would like to drink, I tell him white wine, he disappears back into the house with a murmur of sliding glass, and I'm alone at this table in front of this ocean, a few miles north of Malibu where the wildness begins. The dusk is warm, with just enough humidity to make it cling. I notice an early moon and two long lines of footprints on the sand, going away and coming back.

She sprang, an improbable desert flower, out of the Southwest, thirty-nine years ago. The place was called Happy Jack, but as so often in Arizona it was really no place at all, just a collection of a few hundred people who owned or worked on ranches. Her father was a cowboy named Carpenter, her mother cooked and kept house at the same ranch. Susan believes that her birth was the result of a faulty contraceptive, followed by indecision. They lived in a block of stables converted to servants' quarters and shared with two ranch hands and a middle-aged plowboy. The father was last heard of several years ago in Australia. The mother is dead now, buried by her brother in the Garden of Eden, Tucson. Susan denies that she has Indian blood, but you look at her and wonder. The cheekbones are high, the hair bluish black, and her eyes gaze out at the world in that narrow, slanted Indian way that makes them seem very slightly crossed.

The gaps in Susan's life begin in her childhood; then as now there are sudden blanks and reappearances. When she's three or four her mother becomes ill, and she's sent to live for a while with her uncle who runs a store in Tucson. Then she's back with her parents, but they leave Arizona.

Her father is roping cattle in Nebraska now. She grows up moving farther into space, vastness, clear and lonely air. Today she reads a great deal but she was never properly educated, and the beautiful intent eyes will turn inward if someone mentions a word not too recondite, like "recondite." (She reads, by the way, in definite cycles, the way people do when they search literature for "answers." There was a phase of Tolstoy, Freud and Camus. Today the books on her coffee table are by Hesse, Jung and Aldous Huxley.) Carpenter seems to have been an illiterate. She remembers her mother reading the newspaper out loud to him, and once he took her to Al's Diner in Snake Valley, when her mother wasn't feeling well, and asked her to explain the menu.

A few years of Nebraska, and her parents have separated. She will never see her father again. She goes back to stay with her uncle in Tucson. Then, right after the end of World War II, she and her mother are in New York, sharing the same room at an aunt's apartment. The aunt wears tinted spectacles and tinted hair, works as a checker at a supermarket and lives with the meat and poultry buyer, who drinks beer and winks a lot at Susan. For a few months the two women and the man and the young girl live a life that Susan remembers as like something out of a very long realistic novel written fifty years ago. Amazed to discover how many people still live this way, she goes around in a state of shock. More lonely and displaced even than in Nebraska, she becomes very silent and borrows a great many books from the public library. Mrs. Carpenter polishes up her typing and shorthand that she learned before her marriage and is employed part time at a secretarial service. Occasionally she brings a typing widow home for supper, and cards are played.

They tell Susan she must do more than read books, so she applies to a department store that trains new employees free of charge. Fifteen years old, as tall as she is now, a little over five feet seven, with her smooth black hair and pale skin and the look of exotic distances in her eyes . . . it's not surprising that a photographer notices her and decides she has "possibilities." She soon gets work as a model and is soon quite famous. In the early 1950s her eyes gaze out regularly from the pages of fashion magazines. Today most models look tense and vaguely hostile and wear their clothes like armor, but the taste then was for mystery. They photographed Susan in empty rooms, on the edge of long shadows, leaning against ruined walls or descending a flight of lonely steps. Her past is now in storage—since she sold the big house above Beverly Hills last year she's lived in hotels and rented places—but I remember soon after we met flicking through her bound volumes of *Harper's Bazaar,* with their deliciously absurd shots of Susan in a long black gown, trapped in a kind of cell draped with fishnets, and as a bride, startled and uncertain, in a cage at the Central Park Zoo.

It was during this time she met Charlie Ross, the film producer. A solid, almost ugly and reluctantly charming man, he was about fifteen years older than Susan. Because she was young and beautiful, no one believed that she married him for love. All the usual explanations were advanced. She was frightened of sex and Charlie was a father figure. She was sexually attracted to power and money. She wanted to be a movie star. One even heard that Charlie married *her* because he needed a front. (Male hustlers came late at night to the big house through the back door.) However, you couldn't be in a room with them without noticing that he adored her and that Susan was at least very happy. If he left the room, she looked abandoned.

They entertained a good deal. Like several other writers, I had worked for a few weeks on the script of a movie that was eventually to prove fatal for Charlie, but we became friends and he often invited me to parties. The house was Hollywood-aristocratic, which meant many immaculate rooms, Chagall and Matisse, a projection theater, a library, a pool of course, and an elaborately floodlit garden. Night-blooming jasmine spread its sweet and heavy scent across the patio with its walls of Spanish tile and its brick barbecue like an altar in the center. The Ross parties were fairly large, from forty to seventy people, and they had a casual, assured, slightly outlandish elegance that you find only in California—movie stars, expatriate writers, a visiting film director from India or Italy, a Moroccan princess, a South American diplomat recently involved in an unsuccessful revolution, an old Russian lady who remembered Rasputin, an anthropologist just returned from New Guinea, a ballerina, a marine biologist who talked about dolphins and sharks and how they communicate. With a glitter in her voice, Susan would phone to announce the occasion—"Party time!"—but then, mysteriously, was seldom there to greet her guests. Charlie would do all the honors for an hour or so, then look around and excuse himself and go to fetch her. Once it was almost time for dinner, toward ten o'clock, and Susan hadn't appeared. Charlie had mentioned to me that he'd recently bought a Rouault, and it was hanging in his bedroom, and he wanted me to go upstairs and look at it. I did so without enthusiasm, since Rouault leaves me cold. In his bedroom I found Susan standing in a far corner with a look of complete distraction on her face, yet exquisite in a long white "classical" gown, like something out of an early Isadora Duncan photograph. She wore sandals and a white flower in her hair. She murmured, "Oh, hello!" in a startled way, and rushed out, saying she had to get ready. I was left to stare at a gloomy clown.

A little later, Charlie went to fetch her. She entered the room on his arm, smiling and composed, wearing a different dress. Now she was all in black, and the hair that had been down to her shoulders was piled on top of her head. Until after midnight she was brilliant and drank perhaps two glasses of wine. She wanted to know all about dolphins and India and Rasputin, and everyone remarked how beautiful and *alive* she was. When I was leaving, I couldn't find her. Charlie said she'd gone to bed with a headache.

Charlie began producing films in the late '40s, just when the whole structure of the industry was beginning to crack. For a long time his films and his luck were a little better than most people's, but finally that enormous production of *Tamburlane the Great* lost more than ten million dollars. The parties continued as if nothing had happened, and Susan made her late entrances at his side, until he suffered a heart attack in the middle of a crowded evening. I saw him drop dead in Susan's arms, surrounded by the beautiful and famous.

I never knew Charlie really well but always liked him, partly I suppose because he liked me and partly because he hadn't married an ambitious starlet or a lady who arranged charity balls, but had chosen Susan. He had a dry disenchanted humor, a fascinating inside knowledge of shady political deals and the secrets of the Pentagon and the FBI, and that aura of joylessness which surrounds so many rich, powerful and clever people and makes them truly dangerous. They want you to know they're lonely and vulnerable underneath it all. I'm afraid it was this quality that attracted Susan, for she could talk in the same way about the loneliness of being beautiful. They held on to each other because they saw themselves as two people who had everything and nothing.

At the usual spectacular funeral, as catered as a party, I saw Susan veiled and flowing in black. She stood as if backed into a corner. Two weeks later she'd sold the house and disappeared, saying goodby to hardly anyone. One heard sentimental and outrageous rumors, as one heard them when she married Charlie. She'd gone to stay with her old uncle in Tucson, back to the desert of her childhood and the grave of her mother. She'd taken another name and become a hospital nurse. She was on a yacht in the Mediterranean, with the lover she met a few months before Charlie died.

In fact she rented an isolated house halfway up the mountains above Cannes. She stayed alone there, except for servants, for two months. She read through the Bollingen Foundation editions of *Modern Man in Search of a Soul* and *The Integration of the Personality,* and she studied the I Ching *Book of Changes.* Then she went to Geneva to hear some lectures by Krishnamurti and had a private interview with him. She returned to the house in the mountains and felt, she told me later, that she was achieving a genuine peace. It was broken one night by a sudden unbearable impatience. She got out the car and drove down to the casino at Cannes, where someone recognized her just as she'd won ten thousand francs.

Flicking through the *National Geographic,* I heard a tinkle of bells. Susan approached from the patio. The bells were sewn into the white pants of her suit. Her feet were bare and made no sound. She wore a white hat with an enormous brim that shielded most of her face. I thought, only people who don't really know her can call her Susie or Sue. They not only give themselves away but show a failure of imagination. The beautiful and rich can have nicknames, like Whizzer or Bumbles, but not diminutives.

The wind stirred suddenly. She held on to her hat, gazing at the vase of orange carnations with what seemed to be faintly cross-eyed displeasure.

"Who put those flowers there?"

I remarked that I'd wondered if they were dyed.

"No, surely not. But I can't stand cut flowers, I won't have them in the house. I suppose the new housekeeper . . ." The first reaction had been imperious, but now she seemed hurt and defenseless. Still holding on to her hat, she looked at me, then back at the flowers, made a movement toward the house, retracted it, sank into a chair, got up again. "Would you do me a very great favor? I've already had to explain three things to my new housekeeper today, and I don't want to overwhelm her. Would you take those flowers to the kitchen and tell her that I don't want them and I *never* want cut flowers?"

Her voice was husky, with a faint far-off twang that always sounded to me like an echo from the Great Plains. As I picked up the vase, her imperious manner returned. "But this is terrible! You don't even have a drink yet!"

I told her it was on the way, and carried the vase of orange carnations to the kitchen. A gray, round little woman sat on a counter stool. When I explained, she merely clicked her teeth. "They're so pretty," she said. She placed them in front of herself, reaching out a hand as if to stroke them. I thought her very mild and anxious to please.

Susan was anxious, too, when I got back to the patio. "Did she seem furious? Do you think it's the last straw?"

"No, not at all."

"Thank God." She sank into the chair again, opened the cigarette box, picked up a cigarette. I brought out my lighter but her rather large hand with the silver lacquered nails made a small dismissive gesture, and she lit the cigarette herself. The butler arrived with a bottle of Vouvray in an ice bucket. Without saying a word, Susan and I agreed to be silent while he removed two frosted glasses from the bucket, poured a slow half inch of wine into one of them and handed it to me to taste. I nodded. He nodded gravely back, filled both glasses and withdrew.

Approvingly, Susan watched him go. Then she gave a long sigh of relief. "Now the distractions are over, tell me how you are." Before I could answer she gave me a quick intent glance and said: "You're well. And I love your shirt, I got one just like it the other day."

"I seem to remember a lot of cut flowers up at the old house," I said. "What happened?"

"I took LSD last week." From the flatness in her voice, she might have been announcing she'd just come back from Palm Springs. "You remember Charlie's sister?"

I did; a press agent, divorced, full of bitter energy and reputedly the best poker player in town.

"Well, she gave me a welcome-home party and her son was there, and he's a complete hippie. You can tell he's the real thing because he doesn't wear beads. He'd invited some of his hippie friends and it was interesting, and we talked a lot about pollution and health foods and the orgone box and the end of the world." She laughed. "Really groovy. I'm not making fun of them, by the way, I respect almost everything they say. Anyway, Mike asked if I'd like to come around to somebody's house next day and drop acid with the whole crowd." She laughed again. "I've been in a mood recently to try everything, so I did." She pushed up the brim of her hat. "I think in a way they were kind of hoping I'd freak out, but I didn't, although several of *them* did. A girl got in the orgone box and began screaming and thought she was being buried alive. It was interesting." Her voice sounded reflective. "And my own experience was really beautiful until I made contact with the pain of flowers if you cut them. *That* was intensely vivid! I felt my own heart being torn out. But I kept it to myself, of course." Then, hardly pausing for breath, she changed the subject. She waved at the house. "By the way, isn't it rather hideous here? I've only taken the place for a month and I've got two weeks left. If I can't come to terms with it in that time, I'll have to find somewhere else."

I asked where somewhere else might be. She made a sweeping gesture toward the ocean. "There's always Europe. Except, I've just got back from it."

"And it's not that way. That way is the East."

"Well, there's always the East too." She looked toward it, leaning her elbows on the table. "But I don't know anyone out there." Behind us, the sun slipped quite suddenly over the rim of the mountains. Twilight ended. Blueness fell on everything like a stain. I saw her give a little shiver. "But none of that matters. Not a straw, my friend. Not a hill of beans." She spoke more slowly now, in a low voice, the twang more pronounced, almost grating. "You can guess what Mother's been looking for. Mother's been looking everywhere for Help. And God knows, there's a lot of it around. People and books and drugs and boxes with answers. I'm crazy about them all. And I'd be perfectly all right, I'd be a good sweet girl if I didn't feel that terrible *impatience* I told you about on the phone. It's always worst just when the light goes."

Silver glimmered in the thickening darkness, the plating on the ice bucket and the lacquer on Susan's nails.

"What's the impatience like?" I asked. "What does it make you want to do?"

"Dear God, if I knew, I'd do it." She got up, pressed a switch in the wall. A floodlight went on and made a startling island of the table, chairs, wine, ourselves. Beyond, but now somehow not quite connected, like imperfect process work in a movie, had been placed a beach and an ocean and a molten-looking moon in the sky. "Hideous," Susan said. "Isn't it hideous?" She switched off the light and sat down again. She lit another cigarette. "I think I feel that impatience," she said, "because I've only done two things in my life, and that's not nearly enough. I grew up nobody in the middle of nowhere, then I married Charlie and became somebody in the middle of somewhere."

"What about when you were a model?"

The butler appeared suddenly, like a ghost, and told Susan she was wanted on the telephone. She asked who was calling but he didn't know. She sighed. "I suppose I'd better take it." Getting up, she whispered to me, "They never tell you anything. They love to keep you in the dark."

She came back looking pleased. "Some friends of mine in Palm Beach asking me to go and stay with them. I don't think I want to, but it's good to know if I really find this place unbearable, and I can't find anything else I like, there's *somewhere* to go." Then, without a break: "About being a model. I didn't feel *anything* while I was doing it. It was completely ridiculous, I just did what they said and turned myself into what they wanted. I only *felt* when I was a child, because I was so lonely, and when I was with Charlie."

"What exactly did you feel with Charlie?"

She looked surprised. "I didn't feel lonely. That's what I felt. And now the problem is, I can't seem to find any connection between the first me and the second me. Because I'm neither of them, I suppose. Anyway—" she gazed at the ocean—"there are times when I feel—well, deeply and basically meaningless!"

I said: "Oh, *Susan.*"

She looked surprised again. "But it's true. I am what Jung called a *quantité negligeable.*" She made it sound like *quontitty negliggable.* "I've gone deep enough into Jung to see what's wrong with me, but I can't find the way to put it right. Both he and Krishnamurti say, Don't try and change society—that's the cart before the horse—but change your own nature. I agree with them, but how do you set about doing a thing like that?"

I suggested that if she saw the futility of organized solutions, she must stop looking for them.

It annoyed her. She poured more wine and asked crossly, "But what about *you*? Do *you* feel happy?"

If I said yes, it would be a betrayal. If I said no, it would be depressing. I said, "I feel hopeful."

But she didn't seem to be listening. Something else had occurred to her. "I suppose you think I'm coming out with all this because I can't get over Charlie's death? Well, you're completely wrong. I *have* got over it and I don't even miss him much any more, which is not callous or unfeeling, just the *truth*. A lot of women—" I detected a note of pride— "wouldn't have the courage to look at themselves and admit they're completely *over* the death of a man they . . ." She broke off abruptly. "A man who made them very happy. But I don't have any patience with people who don't have any courage. I just know I'm on the verge of discovering something—about myself and how to live—and maybe all my life so far has only been a kind of preparation. Okay! I'm prepared." She gave me a long look, and the beautiful eyes crossed slightly. "Now what are *you* hopeful *about*?"

"Everything." I shrugged. "And nothing in particular."

"And I'm *prepared* for everything and nothing in particular. What a couple we make, sitting here at the edge of the world."

"I think the situation could be worse."

"You're not taking me seriously."

"You take yourself seriously enough for both of us."

She laughed. Her sense of humor was the more delicious for being buried. But she stopped laughing rather suddenly, and in the silence that followed you could tell she was almost desperately serious. "Of course," she said, trying to keep it light, "it's hopeless expecting anything much in conversation with a writer. It all goes into the printed page. But I'm getting pretty impatient with the printed page, among other things. McLuhan's probably right. It's no good expecting the answer in the Word."

"It's no good expecting the answer."

"I just knew you'd say that!"

"Do you think," I asked casually, "you'll ever love anyone again?"

The question disconcerted her. Finally she said: "Doesn't the answer always lie in something that's never happened to you before?"

This seemed more brilliantly equivocal the more I thought about it. Was it the most direct admission Susan could make of having loved Charlie, or an admission that "love" was an experiment that had failed, or a very concealed way of answering that she *could* love someone because she never had yet?

"Dear God!" She was standing up now. "I'll be late for dinner."

I asked where she was going. She mentioned a producer and his wife who lived in Bel Air, old friends of Charlie's. "I wish I didn't have to. I'm trying to free myself of all that kind of thing, I'd much rather stay with you than eat bad food and see a bad movie . . ." With a tinkle of bells she led the way across the patio. "I really am sorry it's been so short."

"You shouldn't have kept me waiting so long."

She smiled, laid a hand momentarily on my arm. "I'll try not to, next time. If you'll agree to a next time."

"Any time, Susan."

"I love you."

"The answer doesn't lie there."

All the windows in the house were lighted now. Through one I saw a woman, presumably a secretary, tidying some papers at a desk. A maid was starting to draw blinds upstairs. The place was obviously stiff with servants. Susan always found several, instantly, wherever she was.

"You know," she said, "sometimes you seem to be laughing at me. And you're right. But *I'm* going to have the last laugh. There'll be a day when you won't make fun of me any more."

"But promise me you won't become *too* serious."

She stared at me, then her voice rang out unexpectedly loud and harsh. "I really ought to tell you to—!" She broke off with a kind of guilty astonishment. "But I never use words like that," she said. Smiling, she raised her hand in the Peace sign and hurried upstairs.

As I reached the front door I heard her calling my name. I turned back and saw her sitting at the top of the stairs, clutching herself, half in shadow. It wasn't possible to see the expression on her face, but her voice floated down very slowly.

"I'm going to be late for this sickening dinner. That means I'll drive very fast to get there. I've always been a fast driver and I've always been late. Don't tell me there isn't a connection."

"Yes. When you drive very fast, do you notice anything on the way, or is it all just a blur?"

"Nothing at all!" Her voice sounded rather happy. "Just a blur! And if you're always late, you don't really want to go where you're going, anyway." She got up and stretched out her arms, as if on an imaginary cross. "'On the way to where she didn't want to be, she noticed nothing at all.' Maybe I'll put that on my grave."

I heard a laugh and a last tinkle of bells before she disappeared.

Why do we never see enough of the people we truly care about? I wondered about this after you left, and again when I got home from that dinner which was as tiresome as I knew it wd be. Yet I spent four or five hours *there* and less than an hour with you! So in a way you're right to laugh at me. And you're right that things like life and death are not as serious as I make them seem, even though they're all one's got. I would like to see you again very much, very soon. Please call me. Your true friend, Susan.

This note came four days after our meeting. Fog had rolled in from the ocean, which lay half a mile below my house and became invisible and silent. Trees were inklings of themselves. Morning glories closed up and drooped as if dead. It was the kind of day that made you wonder where people were, what they were doing. I called Susan and after the first ring heard a click, then a recorded voice informing me I'd reached a disconnected number. All anyone seemed to know was that she'd left California again. I imagined only one line of footprints on her beach now, stretching a long way away.

Was it somehow extrasensory, that perception of the footprints? Two days later a young painter who lived in the art colony at Mendocino and had been smoking hash half the night went to sleep on the beach. The beaches in the north of California are longer, wider, often completely empty. Waves break higher up there. You can drive for miles along the coast highway and not pass another car or human being. The desert doesn't reach up there. More rainfall occurs and the land is greener. After a storm, along one of the stretches with no house or gas station in sight, you can forget the telegraph wires and imagine yourself in glistening unexplored territory. A bear or an Indian might walk out of the woods.

Sunrise woke the young painter up. It seemed of course indescribably beautiful. He had shoulder-length hair, wore a pair of Levis and a Cossack blouse with an embroidered collar. He began to walk along the beach, and after a while wondered if he wasn't still hallucinating. He found that he was walking parallel to another set of footprints, like an echo of his own. They seemed to stretch away forever. They obsessed him. He thinks he must have walked for a mile and they were still there, at his side. He remembers nothing else except that, just before the footprints turned, he noticed a black car parked off the highway.

The footprints turned toward the ocean, then stopped abruptly. The tide was going out, and on the wet sand lay a pair of gold sandals, a pair of Pucci pants, a white sweater and a white broad-brimmed hat, soaked and drooping now. Still uncertain whether he was hallucinating or not, the painter picked up the sandals and tried them on for size. He remembers being disappointed they were too small. Then he noticed a body floating not far out in the ocean, just beyond where the surf broke.

He said to himself, This is reality after all. A drowned or drowning person lay out there. He would very much have liked to save this person but unfortunately he couldn't swim. There was no one else about. He stood gazing numbly at the ocean with the gold sandals in his hand. He thinks he must have continued to do this for at least two minutes before an extraordinary thing happened. A wave broke farther out than usual and carried the body all the way back to the shore. It turned over as it reached him and rolled naked, face downward, on the sand. A gull swooped low out of nowhere, squawking.

He says he will always remember the groovy surprise of Susan's bare white ass gleaming in the early-morning sun at his feet.

Discovering that Susan was still alive, the painter tried to carry her to the black car. It was too far and she was too heavy for him. So he left her body on the sand. Luckily the keys were still in Susan's car and he drove to the nearest phone booth and called for an ambulance. The newspapers printed a photograph of Susan arriving at the hospital on a stretcher. It was somehow characteristic, at this moment, that with her eyes closed and her black hair matted she should have looked more beautiful than ever and about ten years younger. (Before she was identified, the reports described her simply as a girl.) They pumped the water out of her and for a few hours, as she lay between them, life and death turned out to be serious after all. When she was conscious again, she asked a nurse to telephone Juliet Kappler, her closest friend in Hollywood. Juliet immediately chartered a plane and arrived at the hospital late that night. In the meantime Susan had faced doctors and police with a tired, almost amused composure, telling them she'd gone out for an early-morning swim and been caught in an undertow. There was nothing in her manner or her state of mind, everyone agreed, to suggest she might have tried to drown herself. She made a quick recovery, and three days later went to stay at Juliet's house. It was less than a mile away from the house in which she'd lived with Charlie Ross.

Juliet, a few years older than Susan, was also a widow. Kappler and Charlie Ross had started out as partners in an agency, handling a few "select" movie people, then selling the business to become producers. They were both quickly successful, bought houses close to each other and died within a year of each other. Kappler's occlusion struck him in the middle of the night, in bed, while he was reading a biography of Marlene Dietrich.

With her greenish eyes and white hair worn in flat, Madonna style, Juliet was still a remarkable beauty. She had the look of those English court ladies in seventeenth-century miniatures, everything about her scaled down, delicately straight, giving nothing away. In fact she was the daughter of a famous New York criminal lawyer and became the most elegant and discreetly promiscuous of international lesbians, the kind of woman who turned

Kappler on, as they say; and he was the only man, apparently, who did the same for her. A son was born but the marriage didn't last. For a long time they lived in friendly separation. Kappler gave Juliet the house, then left her most of his money. A week before he died, their son Paul was driving back from a bullfight at Tijuana with a friend. He was nineteen. The car skidded on the freeway in a thunderstorm, went out of control, slammed through the dividing barrier, caused a chain of accidents. Five other cars collided or overturned in the beating rain. Only one person was killed, Paul's friend, but the only part of Paul that survived was his brain. Paralyzed from the neck down, he could still speak and understand what people were saying, but the rest of him was useless, inanimate, like a weed. He could read but was unable to turn the pages of a book. If he slumped sideways while sitting in a chair, he had to be helped upright again. It seemed that he would sit or lie around forever, being fed and taken for drives, watching television and the sky, and that Juliet would read aloud to him until one of them died. In the meantime she'd replaced Kappler. At a private club she met a psychiatrist's daughter, and it became her second marriage.

The house was rambling and secluded, larger than Charlie Ross's, an estate protected by a high wire fence. The grounds had been left to run wild. Passion flowers wreathed themselves around spacious elms, their tropical blooms pushing between thick branches. Ferns and bamboo made a jungle. There was an orchard of apple and citrus trees with ivy spiraling up their trunks. When I rang the bell, a peephole in the door opened and the black housekeeper's face looked warily out. She remembered me and said everyone was on the patio. I walked through the hallway and living room, dark and heavy with paneled walls, beamed ceilings, solid antique furniture, Persian rugs faded just enough to show how authentic they were. The patio was the cultivated part of the grounds, a long brick terrace facing the pool and a gabled guest house. There were canvas chairs and redwood tables, geraniums in painted tubs. A hillside loomed above, dense with ivy. The land sloped away on either side to trees and rustling shadows.

I saw Susan in her usual white hat and pants suit, lying on a chaise longue under an umbrella. Paul had been placed on another chaise longue nearby. He was blond, as his mother had once been, with the same small and chiseled features. He wore a ruffled shirt, tight flowered pants and an Indian headband. His eyes were greenish like his mother's, but glassy and too still, like standing water. Juliet stood in a lemon-colored caftan and matching sunglasses, reading aloud to him. As I appeared, she dropped a paperback volume of stories by Chekhov, placed white indolent hands on my shoulders and kissed me on the cheek.

Susan greeted me rather briefly, then stared at Juliet. "But will he be all right?" Her voice was low and vibrant. I didn't know at first what she was talking about, then she said, "You should have come five minutes later, my friend, and let Juliet reach the end of the story."

I asked what the story was about.

"A young man." She lay back. "He has these strange periods of depression."

"Why are they strange?"

"He doesn't know what causes them."

"It would be stranger if he *did* know." Paul smiled. "Very few people with depressions know what causes them."

She gave him a startled look. "But you've thrown me off the track!"

"You're so easy to throw."

"My son is a tease," Juliet said.

Susan lay back even further. "He thinks about suicide, this young man. The depressions got worse and worse and that's what he thinks about. And yet somehow he *knows* they won't last forever and he won't kill himself. He *seems* to be able to keep going, to live through it all." A hand with silver nails gestured at Juliet. "But will he be all right?"

"I don't know, darling." Juliet shrugged. "I didn't finish the story."

"Relax," Paul said. "It's okay. The joker lives."

"You know this story already?" Juliet asked her son. "Why did you let me read it to you?"

"I've never read it before." Paul half closed his eyes. His voice sounded very patient and sweet. "But I just know, like the character knows, he's not going to do anything as dreary as kill himself."

After this, he became abstracted and hardly spoke. We began to chat of nothing in particular. Susan withdrew to the background but flashed me a look that said *later*. She put on a pair of immense mauve-tinted glasses. Then Lilian came out like a shy youth, hands in the pockets of her jeans, eyes very sharp and alert but not looking at anybody. Tension followed her like a shadow, its presence unmistakable but hard to pin down—something in the way her face, pointed and freckled, refused to smile. She sat on a chair and it became an island, separate from the rest of us, facing away at a slight angle. I thought at first that she resented Susan, then that she was permanently jealous of Paul. Perhaps both guesses were right, but there was something else. How difficult to live in such a beautiful and afflicted household. Lilian couldn't compete with the grace or the grief, so she cast herself in the role of outsider, upstaging with an air of awkward solitude.

If Juliet was aware of any of this, she gave no sign. A long time ago, I supposed, she'd come to terms with the extraordinary by regarding it as commonplace. So, when she talked of anything commonplace, it could seem extraordinary. Over lunch on the patio, while her son lay motionless and stared at the sky, we ate cold chicken, a salad of artichokes, tomatoes and limestone lettuce, pears and cheese, and drank a pitcher of white wine with sliced peaches in it; and Juliet discussed, as if the problem were unique to herself, the injustice of high taxation, which might drive her to sell the house and live in Europe. This led to an attack on the way the government spent its money, which led to the extravagance of landing on a barren moon. The outlook struck her as worse and worse, and superstition intruded. She seriously believed, passing around the huge teak salad bowl, that the cosmos had been disturbed and there'd be a major earthquake quite soon. Lilian objected. "That's quite unscientific," she said. "Maybe so," Juliet said, "but you must admit an earthquake is *overdue*." (Because of the San Andreas fault, earthquake fear is a recurring neurosis in California. This long fracture in the earth's subterranean crust extends for more than two hundred miles below the sunlit state, and nothing can be done about it. Everything else, theoretically, *could* be perfect. But the fault is irremediable, like a wound that will never heal and can always be reopened.) A silence occurred after Juliet's thought of an overdue earthquake, then she brought up a fairly horrible crime committed just last week—"while I was up in Mendocino—" smiling at Susan—"looking after you, darling." At a house practically across the street, as she put it with no intention of irony, a young girl had been brutalized and murdered. She was the daughter of a department-store owner, and her parents were away for the weekend. There were no clues, either to the criminal or his motives.

Another silence occurred. I noticed a single scarlet hibiscus flower floating in the pool. Then, somewhere in the bamboo forest, a blue jay chattered. Lilian helped herself to more salad and Susan considered a cigarette.

"And have you noticed," Juliet went on brightly, "that when there doesn't seem to be a motive, the murder is always much more violent?" Lilian seemed about to object again, but was given no time. "And have you *also* noticed—" the voice went higher, partly for emphasis and partly because there were now two blue jays chattering furiously at each other—"that in most murders these days there doesn't seem to *be* a motive? What has happened to people's motives? If I'm going to be killed, I want to know why." Anyway, it was really sad. She'd met the girl at a party and you hated to see things like that happening to someone so charming and young.

I glanced at Paul. He watched his mother now, his face expressionless, but one of his arms had dropped down and hung limp and swaying. Lilian saw it and got up quickly to place it back at his side. He didn't thank her. Susan was lighting a cigarette and Juliet appeared not to notice.

"They'll find the motive." Susan snapped out her lighter. "And when they do, you can be sure it's hideous. In a way I'd rather not know about it."

Juliet became very alert. "What kind of hideous, darling?"

"Some hell or other. Charlie used to say, It's as if a great many people live in wonderful houses with a ghastly stinking cellar underneath. They never go down there, of course, but once in a while some creature comes up."

And she gave us all a brief, enigmatic smile. As with Juliet, the sunlit talk of violence and terror, even by extension the beautiful cripple on the chaise longue, seemed to act as a pick-me-up. There was no apparent cloud in Susan's sky. She looked still younger and more radiant than I'd ever seen her, pale skin almost translucent and a dark light burning in her eyes.

Lilian said, "Paul, aren't you hungry?"

He nodded. "I'm starving."

"Oh, my angel!" Juliet went over and rested a hand lightly on his forehead. His eyes closed. To Lilian she said, "Let's feed him inside," and to Susan and myself, "I'm sure you have plenty to gossip about." They started to wheel him away, past my chair. He glanced at me and remarked pleasantly, "You listen to Susan and my mother talk and you'd think they never experienced a damn thing in their lives. I call that style."

Susan looked rather astonished, but Juliet smiled and laid her cheek against Paul's face. After a moment, Lilian gave the chaise an abrupt push and they disappeared into the house.

"It's really quite beautiful here, isn't it?" Susan said.

I stared at her, thinking she meant the perfect blue sky, the brightness of the pool and patio, but she went on: "With Juliet. To have gone through all that and be the rock she is."

"The whole set-up doesn't remind you at all of *Ethan Frome*?"

She didn't smile. "Juliet means no harm." Her voice had its low, urgent twang. "And you can't say that about many people." Then she gave me a peculiar look, as if she had a secret of which she was especially proud. "In answer to the question you're dying to ask, I *did* mean to." She picked a slice of peach out of the empty pitcher of wine and nibbled on it.

I wondered why she'd walked into the ocean.

"Yes. Everyone asks that." Susan sounded wistful. "I wasn't really sure at first, then I realized afterwards it all started when I weighed myself on the bathroom scales and found I'd gained four pounds in one week."

"You can't be serious."

"At last I've turned the tables!" Excited, she touched my hand. "At last you're more serious than I am! But it's true anyway. When your life is basically no good, the trouble starts over the most ridiculous things. If something truly dreadful had happened to me last week, I'd never have behaved so foolishly. But this weight thing really got to me. It wasn't the first time I'd found myself gaining, and I started thinking, Maybe being fat is really *you*, maybe you're an essentially fat person, your lovely body's just a

32

fraud and now it comes out! Yes, you'll grow old and heavy and disguise yourself in long robes. All fat people, especially women, are deep down very sad. *It weighs them down.* I thought of all the tiresome lonely women I knew, putting on weight or struggling to take it off. And it got to a point. So I ended up taking a couple of tranquilizers, getting out the car and driving north."

The housekeeper appeared with a tray. "Thank you, Bessie, we are finished, take it all away," Susan said, and went straight on. "At first it helped, that beautiful coast highway, the redwoods, driving high above the ocean crashing down on the rocks. When it got dark I checked in at some nowhere motel just before San Francisco. In the room, it began getting to a point again. And the TV didn't work, another ridiculous thing that really depressed me. I went out and ate some dinner, came back and wept, and took a sleeping pill. There were dreams I don't want to tell you about. Next morning I got up early and drove on. Everything got quite impressive but too desolate. When it was dark again I bought a bottle of brandy, headed out a few miles from wherever I was, parked somewhere above a beach and decided to sleep in the car. I finished nearly all the brandy and took a couple of sleeping pills. A wind got up. There were all kinds of strange sounds in the distance—birds, animals, trees, I don't know what. And then more dreams. When I woke, sometime before dawn, I was shaking all over and more depressed than ever in my whole entire life. I felt—well, suicidal." The housekeeper removed her empty coffee cup. Susan said, "Oh, Bessie, could you bring us some more coffee?" and turned back to me. "I looked back and tried to remember being happy, and I could, but there was no connection. I looked forward and you can imagine. I changed into some nice clothes and made myself up rather well. I did all of that in the car, just as the sun rose. Not thinking. Like taking down dictation. Then I got up and walked down to the beach. Then into the water. Same thing. Obeying orders!" She grimaced. "And it was somewhat colder than winter, my friend."

She got up and walked slowly back to her chaise longue. I noticed how thin she looked. She settled herself under the umbrella. "I love the sun, you know, but I'm allergic to it. Isn't that unfair?"

"Yes. After I got your note," I said, "which was very sweet of you, I called. But the number was disconnected."

"I paid off all the servants too, before I left. The only thing I knew was I'd never come back to that house. But now I want to tell you about the important part."

"All that driving around and panic and bad dreams and walking into the ocean wasn't the important part?"

She shook her head. "I've come to realize—" and she looked suddenly astonished, as if realizing it all over again—"that fate must be on my side."

"Because you're still alive?"

She nodded.

"But is fate on anyone's side?"

"It's on mine," Susan said. "And you know what it's usually like. Late at night, at an intersection where there hasn't been any traffic for at least fifteen minutes, two cars arrive at the same moment." Her eyes crossed slightly. "One of the drivers is careless or drunk or something, and gets killed." A sharp intake of breath. "That's what fate is usually like." Then she leaned back. "Charlie taught me that," she said quietly. "We have to be very careful."

The housekeeper returned with more coffee. "Bessie, you're a dear." Susan flashed her a brilliant smile and poured for both of us. "And that's why it's so mysterious," she went on. "All kinds of marvelous people die, like my husband and Juliet's, and the Kennedys, and Marilyn Monroe, and Martin Luther King, but for some reason when *I* decided to walk away from it all, this hippie artist was wandering along the beach stoned out of his mind and managed to save my life."

"Did you talk to him afterwards?"

She nodded. "He came to visit me in the hospital. He brought me a flower and we rapped, as he put it, about Jung and astrology. He hadn't read Jung—hardly any of them read, you know—but he'd heard that Jung dug astrology, as he put it, and we talked about our signs. I'm Gemini and he's Aquarius, which means we're perfectly compatible, made for each other. Isn't that quite a coincidence? It started me thinking about predestination and fate. If my life was saved, that ought to mean it's worth saving."

I thought of lives that had been saved and didn't seem to be worth it, but to have brought this up would have been graceless. Besides, it was rare to see someone survive that most humiliating failure, an unsuccessful attempt at suicide, with no vestige of shame or guilt. Susan seemed to be glowing in its aftermath, as if she'd just had a wonderful sexual experience.

Then, for a moment, the light went out of her face. "Of course, I'm really on the spot now and my impatience is worse than ever. Because I'd damn well better find out *why* my life is worth saving."

Now it's another large house, in another section of the hills. Susan has asked me to take her to a party there. As we drive up, a cop springs to open the door of my car. He asks who we are. Susan looks alarmed, but I recognize the cop from another party and know he's only rented. If you want to appear very exclusive, or are truly paranoiac about gate crashers, you can rent these people. They wear a uniform deceptively close to the real one and carry guns.

"Sometimes," Susan remarks, "I feel I'm living in a rented universe."

She's already told me the host is called Taube, but she doesn't know whether this is his first or last name. She *does* know that he's the son of a German millionaire and supposes the money comes from armaments, because in Germany no one makes millions from anything else. Since she's never met him, I ask how she happened to be invited. She looks surprised and says, "He called me, of course."

I make a small bet that I'll recognize Taube at once. He will have long hair and wear Levis with a very beautiful and expensive shirt. Most millionaires have one son who breaks away from the family and the business, mixes with "creative" people, mainly from the movies and pop music, and wears his half-casual, half-formal costume at parties all over the world. I lose the bet, because as we come in there's a group of five young men all dressed this way. All sons of millionaires, of course, but the one I think is Taube turns out to be Latta Brothers Coffee. They stand around a man in his cups who can only be a journalist. He is telling them, in the kind of loud, desperate voice that dares them not to listen, that he just got back from Biafra. He describes starving children and hideous brutality. They nod, believe, look at each other, and clearly wish he would shut up. A row of chandeliers quivers. They have dimmed flickering electric bulbs that simulate candlelight. Waiters move around with trays of drinks and the phonograph plays the Rolling Stones. A few couples dance, though not really with each other.

Susan listened to the man's account of a village massacre with a curious intent expression, then turned to me. "Dear God, it's Bill. I wonder who let him in?"

Bill saw her at the same moment, broke off and came over. His walk was too carefully steady. Dark and stocky, and probably quite good-looking a few years ago, he now had that typecast seediness of actors in movies with a newspaper background. He stared at Susan, then kissed her hand. She withdrew it quickly. You could feel an intimate hostility between them.

"Well. Susan."

"How are you, Bill?"

"I feel I have no right to be alive. I just got back from Biafra." He took another Scotch from a passing tray. "I guess you've been feeling the same way, too. Didn't you just do the old Joan Crawford movie routine and walk into the ocean in evening dress?"

A total, appalled silence. Only the tinkle of chandeliers.

Susan smiled. Her eyes looked faintly crossed. "No, I took off my clothes first."

She turned away, but Bill caught her arm. Then Taube came forward, a big and blandly handsome boy with a radiant tan obtained on the ski slopes rather than the beach. He had a mop of golden hair, wore a thin silver necklace and bracelet, and a mauve see-through shirt open to the navel. He shoved Bill in the stomach and told him to get out.

"Please . . ." Susan turned back. "You don't have to do that. It's all right. I don't mind."

"You don't matter," Bill said.

I noticed a row of girls, loafing against a nearby wall, wearing caftans and ponchos. They stared. They looked temporary and ignored. Perhaps they were rented, too.

Susan smiled again at Bill. "You may be right. There have certainly been times when I felt I didn't matter."

"If you went to Biafra you'd know you'd never matter again."

"Oh, come off it," I said. "What a stupid idea that the only reality in the world is where people are dying. You can't put someone down just because they're *not* being tortured or raped or starved."

"Yes, you always *did* boast about having seen people suffer." Then a look of genuine concern came over Susan's face. "And Biafra's lost that war. Why must you always back losers?"

"Jesus!" He gave a rather theatrical laugh. "Hollywood! California! Everything they say about this place is true. Can't any of you here face anything outside yourself?"

Susan looked at Bill as if he were a lost cause, then asked me again: "But who let him in?"

There were more people staring now. The girls huddled together. Only the dancers at the other end of the room took no notice.

Taube and another young millionaire's son hustled Bill out. He swore loudly, shouting all the usual words, then apologized. They began arguing in the hallway.

Everyone nearby was watching Susan. She took out a cigarette. Somebody snapped his lighter open but she waved it away and lit the cigarette herself. Her hands were completely steady. She murmured to me, "It's really a shame about Bill and his drinking." Then Taube came back and said how sorry he was, and she told him not to be silly, and they laughed and introduced themselves and began discussing people I didn't know who lived in Switzerland, Majorca and Rome.

Later in the evening I went to the bathroom. The door was half open, the room itself in darkness. A silhouette with its head in its hands sat on the toilet and made a groaning sound. Then Bill looked up and saw me. "Okay, take a piss," he said and got up. "I was just sitting here." There was a stench of stale vomit. He remained in the doorway and asked how long I'd known Susan.

"Three or four years," I said.

"Not as long as I've known her. We nearly got married." He made another groan. "Right before she met old Charlie Ross. She threw me over for that rich old man."

"Well, better that than Biafra."

He laughed. "Was I really a swine out there?"

"Yes."

The idea seemed to please him. "Yes." He laughed again. "What a ding-a-ling!"

"You?"

"Susie. Would you believe, the horniest lady I ever knew? And settled for a rich old man?"

The stench was really overpowering. I flushed the john, walked out past Bill and said, "They asked you to go home." In the living room floated another odor, sweetish and heavy. At the far end I saw Susan surrounded by all the sons of the millionaires, and a movie actor with long sideburns, and I think a rock group, and various girls. She sat on a high-backed chair and it looked like a throne. Most of the others squatted or lay on the floor. I felt I was approaching a ritual. Joints were being passed around but Susan never took one. I could see that she didn't need to; there was a kind of transfixed, drugged alertness in her eyes. They turned a passionate fraction inward. "That's the whole point!" she was saying to Taube, who stood beside her and scratched his bare chest. "Loneliness doesn't consist of not having friends. Loneliness has nothing to do with that! It's being unable to express your deepest feelings and most private thoughts."

Taube's jeans were much too tight to hide his erection. The others didn't appear to notice it. They all nodded, faces young and vague and content. A girl murmured, "Oh, out of sight."

"It's having ideas that other people don't understand, and seeing things they never see." The twang crept into Susan's voice. "That's why the loneliest people are artists and clairvoyants and madmen."

A Bronx cheer sounded farther down the room. "Which are you, baby?"

We all looked up. Bill stood beneath a flickering chandelier, vomit stains on his jacket.

"If I'm anything, I'm mad," Susan said. "But not dangerous."

He didn't answer. The girls discussed loneliness wistfully among themselves. They decided that Susan was right. They mentioned Van Gogh, Nijinsky, Garbo.

Taube smiled. "All you're saying is that anybody's lonely if he's superior or different."

"But you mustn't be a snob about it." Susan leaned toward him. "I'm not saying loneliness is so great, just explaining how it happens. Of course it would be wonderful if there was a way of being unique without feeling lonely."

"If there was, how would you *know* you were unique?"

She shrugged. "One more question to which there's no answer."

Taube grasped her hand and held on to it. Across the room, Bill gave a loud belch and went out.

"There's a thing inside us." Susan gazed wonderingly at Taube's hand enclosing hers. "It says, I may want to love you, to reach out and touch you, but I can't. I have to go my own way."

He didn't release her hand, and she didn't try to withdraw it. In a way I can't explain, she didn't accept the gesture, either. The expression on her face was polite and a little concerned, as if Taube were a stranger and she was unsure whether or not to tell him he had a smut on his face. Later, she came over to me, laid a hand briefly on my arm and said not to worry about driving her back to Juliet's house. I nodded. "It's really quite a nice party," she said, sounding surprised. "I didn't think it would be. I almost suggested we ax it and have a quiet dinner together, but I'm glad now that we came. By the way, I probably needn't ask you this, but please don't tell anyone."

"About not driving you home?"

She frowned slightly. "No. About Bill. I'm sure you guessed, anyway."

"He told me."

She stared. "How? Where?"

"In the john."

"What a suitable place."

Taube appeared, standing behind her. She glanced at him, then back at me, and gave a sudden laugh. I asked what was so funny and she said, "Oh, you *know*. Don't you *know*?" Then, as sometimes happened, she stopped laughing as abruptly as she began, and I knew she was serious about something, and so did she, but neither of us could give it a name.

> Dear Susan, Aren't you too intelligent and beautiful and rich to worry about the things most people worry about, such as growing old and unloved or destitute or overlooked, and you insist it's not Charlie dying and you got laid last night, so what *is* the matter? . . .

I started to compose this letter in my head, but of course I never wrote or sent it. For a while Susan and I stayed out of touch with each other. This meant nothing except that we were both living in Southern California and, as the saying goes, in different worlds. There are so many different worlds here, separated by distances of twenty or thirty miles, that people live in tribes rather than as a community. The world outside is something you see from a car. Members of the same tribe meet regularly, but if you belong to different ones it usually takes some kind of pow-wow to bring you together, a rite or celebration involving marriage, death, visiting chieftains, festivals, victories.

Since Charlie died, Susan had been without a tribe. She wasn't banished; she dropped out. The houses of Bel Air that belonged to producers and executives whose fathers and uncles had "founded the industry" were still open to her. But she very seldom now visited these fortresses with their collections of French painting and long polished dining tables and movies screened punctually after dessert and coffee. The Bel Air wives, miffed when she started refusing invitations, decided that Susan as a widow was not doing the right thing. They were sorry for her and understood that grief could make a person briefly antisocial, but her aloofness was becoming a great mistake. Maybe if they subtly phased her out, she would realize it.

I thought at first that Taube might have introduced Susan to a new tribe, but it never happened. He left California. One day I saw an item in a weekly news magazine about a party he'd given in Rome. It reminded me of Susan and I decided that too much time had passed without us at least talking to each other, so I called Juliet. We chatted for a few minutes, then I asked to speak to Susan. Juliet sounded surprised. Didn't I know she'd left California again? "I felt somehow you were one of the people she'd have said goodby to." I asked if by any chance she'd gone to Rome. Juliet got the point immediately and said that after the night of that party she was sure Susan never saw Taube again. She didn't know where Susan had gone: possibly to New York, although the day she left she'd had an invitation to join some friends on a yacht in the Caribbean.

"Anyway, thereby hangs a tale. If you want to drop by for a drink, I'll tell it."

The afternoon was overcast and cool. Beyond the French windows I saw the patio with its umbrellas collapsed over tables and little eddies of steam rising above the pool. In the muted light, Juliet's living room had a displaced and waiting quality, an inner echo for which I caught myself listening. Juliet standing by the phonograph and Paul lying on the couch didn't live there, they only haunted the place. All life and color were contained in the brilliant flowers scattered everywhere in vases—marigolds, roses, chrysanthemums. Then Mozart began and Juliet came toward me, finger to her lips. She took my arm and we walked past Paul. His eyes were closed but he wasn't asleep; he was listening and she didn't want him to be disturbed. We went into the den at the back. She closed the door and told me her tale.

About a week after Taube's party, Juliet was sitting on the patio reading aloud to Paul. It was mid-morning and Susan had slept late. When she appeared, she seemed unusually preoccupied. She gave Juliet a rather wan smile and went to sit by herself, sipping coffee. She picked up the newspaper, put it down again with a sigh. She moved restlessly to another chair. Juliet asked if anything was the matter. Susan said, "I had a dream I don't want to tell you about. But I woke up with a terrible impatient feeling. I hope you won't find this ridiculous, but I'm too cut off from a lot that's going on in the world and I want to come face to face with a kind of life that's entirely new and different." Juliet asked what kind of life this might be. Susan became breathless and anxious and talked rather wildly of truths that had to be acknowledged and of her need to be shocked and outraged. Then, veering off, she said that while she'd never do "charity work," in the sense of organizing galas and premieres, because it was false and empty and women sat on committees like that purely out of social obligation, she would like to *confront* people who actually needed charity, who were desperate and bitter and diseased. Had Juliet ever thought of smelling the breath and touching the open wounds of such people? Could she imagine their garbage and anger and overflowing toilets? Juliet supposed that she could if she tried. "Then go on," Susan said. "Tell me." Reluctantly, Juliet described bugs climbing up walls and out of mattresses, and the stench of decomposed food and filthy bodies. Paul said he could think of worse things. He told Susan about rats attacking a sick baby, dead old women left to rot in upstairs rooms, a tapeworm longer than the intestine in which it lived. But for Susan, nothing they could describe was as bad as her dream. "I dream of these hideous things I've never seen. If I go out and see them, won't I stop dreaming about them?" At the last dinner party she'd attended in Bel Air, the son of the house was a student who'd formed a volunteer organization called "Assist." With one or two helpers he drove to the slums of Los Angeles twice a week in a truck with a mobile telephone. People came to the truck and were given free coffee and cookies and told how they could be assisted. The student telephoned doctors, lawyers, employment agencies and whoever else might be of help. "I'm going to call him now," Susan said. "And if he lets me assist him, he'll have no idea how he's assisting *me*."

The student was presumably stunned but grateful for any offer. It was agreed that Susan should go out with the truck on his next trip and serve free coffee and cookies. He would pick her up at nine o'clock. That morning she was up at dawn and spent several hours trying to decide what she should wear. She emerged looking as she usually did, a broad-brimmed hat shielding half her face from the world. She'd chosen a white linen suit that she didn't care if she never wore again, being convinced it would get spattered with grime and swill. The student arrived in old Levis and a sweat shirt. He gave Susan a deadpan look and said, "Let's go." The destination that day was a downtown slum not far from the city jail. The student parked his truck and switched on a tape machine that played rock-'n'-roll music. Soon about twenty people had gathered around, some curious, some drunk, some wanting definite assistance, and some just interested in a free cookie. An elderly couple began complaining about each other to the student, the woman showed a greenish bruise between her shoulder blades, and Susan put on a pair of dark glasses and filled Dixie cups from the coffee urn. The others watched her steadily—a Negro laborer with a seamed and stubbled face who held up a hand of which three fingers were broken, a mother instructing her little son to open his mouth and show his swollen bleeding gums, a Mexican pointing to his bare stomach with an unhealed knife wound across it. A wino lurched past, almost touching Susan, and her hands trembled a little as they arranged cookies on a cardboard plate. Luckily the brim of her hat and the dark glasses hid most of her face, or they would all have seen the white terror in it and been themselves frightened, contemptuous, maybe even violent. As it was, they accepted coffee from a lady they knew to be elegant and guessed to be beautiful, whose mouth parted in what they took to be a smile and whose hands with their silver lacquered nails shook slightly out of what they thought was eagerness. Afterward, Susan told Juliet that the wounds and ugliness and vacant despair, the tales of hard luck and injustice, the gray pitted skin of a heroin addict's arm, the goiter on an old man's neck, the woman shouting because she could hardly hear, the swollen veins and leaking infections produced no feeling of pity or repulsion, only a humiliating fear. The shock treatment she'd devised for herself was only making her more frightened than ever. All that kept her from running away was the student so calmly telephoning a hospital, a dentist, a drug clinic, and a voice inside her that said she *wanted* this fear and deserved it. While she continued handing around coffee and cookies, fantasies tore through her mind; she could see the crotch of a young Negro's pants swelling directly at her, she heard obscenities when a dim old hobo muttered soundlessly to himself, and the boy showed his diseased mouth only to stick out his tongue and waggle it in her face. She was more alone and threatened than she'd ever been in her life. She could only pray for the time to pass quickly and tell herself that if she didn't hold on she'd be mocked and kicked and stoned.

Then after a few hours the work became mechanical and her fear seemed to subside. If she didn't enjoy what she was doing, she was at least vaguely proud to be doing it. Around the middle of the day the student offered her a sandwich, but she wasn't hungry. Later on, she even handled a case herself. She called her own lawyer on behalf of a man who claimed his last employer owed him money. The lawyer appeared to think that Susan being down there was strange but wonderful and promised to take on the case without charge. Contact with someone she knew, and approval from him, made her feel much better. She put down the mobile phone and realized she hadn't smoked a cigarette all day. She lit one now and the luxury seemed extraordinary.

In the early evening, when the light was just beginning to grow soft and the air felt less gritty, she became aware that a pair of eyes, dark and wrinkled like prunes, had been fixed upon her for some time. They belonged to a small, dirty, trembling old woman, almost a dwarf. The head was much too large for the body and the eyes themselves seemed to reflect a stunted, hopeless mind. Instinct had warned Susan not to offer this person a cup of coffee, then she reminded herself that she'd found something approaching courage. How ridiculous to be afraid of someone just because she was ugly. Another look at the eyes and she saw a desperate appeal in them. They surely belonged to someone who imagined herself a child but had looked in the mirror and seen gray hair, raddled skin and dreadful withered breasts. Susan filled a Dixie cup with coffee and handed it to the woman, who took it without a word, lifted it to her mouth and made a violent, wobbling grimace. Susan was about to ask if she would like sugar, when the creature became transformed, diabolical, uttered a piglike snort and flung the coffee straight into her face. Fortunately it wasn't very hot and most of it went on the brim of Susan's hat and splashed her dark glasses.

The tape machine was pounding out its music. Without a word Susan turned away and ran up the street. Coffee dripped down her face and neck. The student called after her, but she only ran faster. She knew that people were staring and pointing at her, then a helicopter whirred above her head. She came to on a sidewalk bench at a bus stop. The advertisement on its back said, 16 DAYS IN SPAIN, $225.00, AIR FARE NOT INCLUDED! They sent her home in a cab. Juliet saw her come into the house, walking very slowly. She shook her head and locked herself in her room.

After a while, Juliet became anxious. She knocked on the door and got no answer. She looked in through the window and saw Susan inert on the bed, apparently asleep. She had taken off only her shoes and her hat. Remembering the ocean at Mendocino, Juliet climbed in and shook her awake. Susan was groggy but all right, and said she'd taken only a couple of sleeping pills.

"Sometimes she throws me," Juliet said. "She was much more disturbed by what had happened than when she tried to drown herself. I tried to explain it wasn't her fault, this time *she* hadn't done anything foolish at all, she was trying to be nice to that poor old lunatic. She gave me a strange look and said, 'Don't you see, that makes it much worse? Now there is nothing to be done.' She was determined to run off and hide as soon as possible. When she was leaving for the airport, and saying goodby, she got this phone call inviting her to join these people on a yacht. I said for God's sake, darling, this time go off and *enjoy yourself,* somewhere you *belong.*"

When the telephone rang, a woman's voice with an English accent said, "Mrs. Ross's secretary here. Mrs. Ross is so sorry she can't come to the phone herself, but hopes you'll come over and see her tomorrow. Shall we say three o'clock?" Here's something new, I thought. In the past I'd known Susan elusive and unpunctual, but never this grand. "Shall we say three-thirty?" I asked.

It was a recent, completely isolated house on the edge of a cliff overlooking the ocean. Two miles farther north than Susan's last beach house, a little deeper into the wilderness. You reached it by a turn-off from the coast highway. A sign announced, PRIVATE ROAD. A car was parked outside, with a chauffeur at the wheel. To enter the house you had to pick up a wall telephone and say who you were, then an electronic buzz occurred and the gate swung open. A maid told me, "Mrs. Ross thought you might like to wait on the deck." I followed her through a large, plain, sand-colored living room that reminded me of a motel. Beyond it was a sun deck enclosed in glass. Bleached canvas chairs surrounded a glass-topped table with the same silver cigarette box and a pot planted with wild flowers. They had a dry herbal scent and the look of mountainside survivors, stringy and yellowed.

To my surprise Susan appeared almost at once. After a few weeks in the Caribbean sun she looked almost ecstatically pale, and very thin, and very young. (It seems to me now that from the time that she walked into the ocean, until I never saw her again, Susan looked younger. It was the kind of youthfulness that had its own secret.) She wore sandals and a plain smocklike dress with a skirt ending above the knees. No make-up except for a touch of bluish eye shadow, and only the gentlest of lines in her face. She always made immediate contact with a person through her eyes, and when they rested on me now, just perceptibly turning inward, I thought I saw a remote flicker in their blackness, like the shadow of a shade.

I asked how she enjoyed the Caribbean and she said, "Oh, I believe it was beautiful."

"Now what does that mean?"

"I never left the boat. I discovered that I really don't care to travel any more. And I was only there, you see, *not* to be anywhere else." When she left Juliet's house and boarded the plane to New York, she'd been completely undecided what to do. Disembarking at Kennedy Airport, she entered the Arrivals area and knew at once she couldn't continue into the city. So she called her friends in Palm Beach and said she'd love to join them, then sat by herself in a corner of the cocktail lounge to wait for the next flight to Miami. "I didn't really want to go, but there was nothing else to do. They're charming and generous people, but they never ask *why*—you know what I mean? Still, they were tactful and left me alone whenever I wanted." Susan leaned her forehead against the glass wall and looked out at the ocean and the sky. "This is such a beautiful time of day," she said. "And it's not quite true I don't like to travel. There's one place I go to all the time. Will you come with me?"

She looked very pleased when I said I'd like to, and hurried back into the house. She returned in about ten minutes, and as far as I could see had only tied a scarf around her head and put on a pair of dark glasses. We got into the car waiting outside, and the chauffeur obviously knew where to go, since she didn't speak to him. As we turned onto the coast highway and Susan huddled deep into the back, it occurred to me that she might have decided to have practically nothing more to do with the world. The secretary who made her appointments, the chauffeur who waited with the car, the electronic gate were symptoms not of grandeur but of alarmed withdrawal.

She seemed to be reading my thoughts, because she gave a low, sudden laugh and remarked as we passed a Malibu supermarket that her new housekeeper was wonderful, she did all the shopping and took care of everything that involved outsiders, such as laundry and getting her phone number changed. (It was being changed tomorrow. "Too many people know it already.") I asked if she went anywhere at all these days, apart from wherever we were going now. She looked doubtful, as if trying to remember, and explained how few people she cared to see any more, and then only at their house or hers. She laughed again. "Oh, but I went to a restaurant last week." It had a back entrance and one could slip in quickly past the kitchen and be seated at a dark booth in the corner before anybody knew she was there. I wondered who was granted the favor of a public rendezvous, and she seemed surprised. "I didn't go *with* anyone, I just felt like having dinner somewhere that night." When she wanted to buy clothes, her secretary made a private appointment with the man who designed them for her. And she'd even given up driving a car because she felt more protected with a chauffeur.

One thing occurred to me. "Susan, you used to go to the movies quite a lot."

"That's no problem. My secretary can always get a print of anything I want to see, through one or other of Charlie's old friends, and I have my own projector now and I run it myself."

At Topanga Canyon we turned off the highway and began to climb into the hills. One more thing occurred to me. I wanted to ask Susan about sex, but I didn't know how. If it still interested her, I supposed she could arrange for it somehow. In Southern California there is no necessity or luxury that can't be delivered.

The car followed the winding road through Topanga village. As we neared the top of the pass, signs of human habitation dwindled. The air felt rarer and higher. Up here the landscape becomes almost savage; it might be Greece or the true, secret interior of Provence. You expect a flock of goats to wander across the road. Everything appears luscious and barren at the same time, wild flowers overrun the earth and tall, burdened pines stretch above it, but the mountains are scarred-looking and desolate and the gorges very deep. Near the top the chauffeur made a sharp turn on a narrow road that climbed much more abruptly. For a minute we were tilted toward the sky like passengers in a jet beginning its ascent. Then we reached a small plateau. Farther along I saw two derelict cabinlike houses. The road was thick with dust and I asked Susan where it led. Nowhere at all, she said. The houses were uninhabited. Nobody came here. The car stopped; she took off her dark glasses and got out. We walked together along a shelf of land that dropped steeply away on two sides, plunging down to the gorges and rising again to more mountains. Behind us the road twisted back to the Pacific, and in front, beyond a lower range of hills, lay the edge of the desert. There was no hint of a huge city only twenty miles away. A few hawks wheeled overhead, almost in slow motion.

Susan moved ahead of me with her long model's stride, walking very close to the drop of the land. "You get a feeling up here," she said, "like going back to the beginning of the world. Wasn't the beginning something desolate and hidden like this?" She stopped and dug her foot into the hard, dusty soil. "And can you *prove* that anyone has ever trodden on this particular piece of earth before?" She told me that she came here almost every day, walked a little and sat for an hour or two, watching the late-afternoon light change and slip away, the outline of mountains grow darker, the gorges deeper, the few houses sprinkled about in the distance vanish into shadow. Then she showed me some wild flowers and wanted me to smell them. Their perfume was acrid and fierce, like those on her sun deck. "They have the smell of time," she said. Her eyes no longer flickered, they were black and stony. She gave one of her quick laughs and asked if I thought she might be going crazy.

I remarked that she was living like quite a few other people here, only more so. After all, it's so easy. There are plenty of houses large and isolated enough to guard you from everything except the hills and the ocean. You can listen to all the music in the world in your bedroom, and if you need a reminder of the human condition, you have only to turn on TV. I said that up to a point I liked this way of living myself, I preferred the marketplace to lie around the corner rather than just outside my window. Then I said something about believing in contemplation and in solitude; they were necessary stations along the way, but I wanted to know where her way was leading. After she'd walked and gazed at clouds and mountains, and smelled time in flowers, and frightened herself by thinking of all the cruelty in the world, what did she do but return home and eat her supper and read a book which made her puzzle even more over the state of her soul? She smiled. "I get terribly impatient and take a sleeping pill and start all over again next morning, my friend." Since she'd first felt this impatience, I asked, that night in the south of France, and she'd started living this way, did she feel she'd come any nearer to where she wanted to be?

Susan looked thoughtful. Finally she said, "No." A pause. "Of course, I don't really know where it is I want to be." Another, longer pause. "In the meantime, I'd rather be where I am than anywhere else."

"What about the world? Other people? That's really all over?"

"Yes, of course."

"Why? Not just because an old woman threw a cup of coffee in your face."

"That's not enough? You want something even more horrible to happen to me?" I saw her eyes flicker. "I'm just not capable of facing that kind of *evil* again."

I wondered if the old woman was really as bad as that, as bad as evil. "Call her mindless, or gratuitous, or—"

"But that's what evil is! It's exactly that!" On her pale cheeks, patches of color appeared briefly. "To *plan* to do something cruel or wrong is nothing at all. It's easy. The real test comes when you give way to your instincts, you can't control them, and they show what you *really* are. Most people have instincts like that old woman, so I don't want anything more to do with them."

We strolled for a while in silence. The hawks wheeled overhead; there was no sound anywhere. She sat on a ledge of rock and gazed at the mountains. "In Arizona," she said, "my father took me to a rodeo once. Before it began we had to worship the flag. Imagine, just an ordinary rotten cruel little rodeo, those men trying to bully those animals, and the dust getting in your mouth and eyes, and we had to pray and say how much we loved our country. Still, it wasn't as bad as Nebraska. In *Nebraska*—" she twanged the word—"they'd stand around watching a bull mount a cow, they'd laugh and make jokes and cheer it on, then expect little girls like me to be white as snow. I never saw a man, not even my father, take off his shirt in front of me! I knew he *did* take it off, though, in front of my mother, because that's when they locked their door. Just like the bull and the cow. But why did nobody cheer *them* on? . . ." She broke off, looking rather surprised. "Dear God, what am I talking about?"

"You're rapping, Susan."

She laughed. "Right. I'm trying to explain why I used to hate all that open space. So *much* of it! So *few* people! And no one you could . . ." She stared at the mountains again. "I used to look *beyond* all that open space for something I thought I wanted. You know? Cities and real life?" She laughed again, more harshly. "Well, now I'm sitting here and thinking, If only there *wasn't* anything beyond this open space, how perfect it could be. Isn't that ridiculous? I'm still *wanting.* I can't completely kick the habit. And yet I *know* that wanting things just draws you into the horror outside . . ." There was an ache in her voice. "Charlie understood. He knew how important it was that nothing should ever *happen* to me. And it never did, and I was so happy. But when there's only one of you, it's a little boring sometimes, nothing happening." Then, after a moment, she cheered up. "Still, I've only got two choices, haven't I? To be bored or frightened. And I prefer the first."

"All the same—"

"Yes, I know!" She touched my arm. "It's really a waste and a pity, and the *world*—" she mentioned its name in a flat and remote way, as if discussing a place that was really somewhere else, in which she'd heard that people lived— "the world has some wonderful and beautiful things in it, as well as . . . Yes, I know. Sometimes I feel an idiot for not appreciating . . . I wonder exactly what happened . . . And every time I can't really explain it I feel that terrible lonely thing . . ." She broke off again and suddenly beat the rock with her fist. "Are you familiar with the works of G. K. Chesterton?"

"Here and there."

"Well, I'm not even here and there, except for one little thing he wrote. Charlie told me about it. And it's so exactly what I feel that I never want to read anything else he's written, or anything about him. It could only be disappointing." The light was fading quickly now. There was that pause in everything before dusk fell. In the blurred air her face was that of a girl of sixteen. She spoke in a hushed, breathless voice, nursing her fist, looking toward the west where the ocean lay. *"If a man went westward to the end of the world he would find something—say a tree —that was more or less than a tree, a tree possessed by a spirit. If he went east to the end of the world—"* and she looked toward the shadowy desert now, her fist over her mouth, the words coming through clenched fingers—*"he would find something else that was not wholly itself—a tower, perhaps, of which the very shape was wicked."*

I said, "That's pretty spooky."

She gave a shiver. There was something luxurious in the gesture, a hint of pleasure in the fear. Then she got up and walked toward the car. In the strange light, it was a shape not looking wholly itself.

This time I wrote and mailed a letter:

Dear Susan, I was thinking about everything you said yesterday. The first time I saw you after Charlie died, you didn't know what to do with your life, or what you wanted—but the door was still open. You said you hoped to discover something. Yesterday you talked as if you'd discovered exactly what to do with your life—not to live it. And the door closed. There's a hideous smug quality about proverbs, and maybe about people who quote them, but this one sticks in my mind and won't go away, so I have to get rid of it by sending it on to you. It's about the girl who never dances because she says there's never a band that knows how to play . . .

The English voice said: "Mrs. Ross's secretary here. Please hold on for a moment. Mrs. Ross is coming to the phone." She made it sound like a very special occasion.

I heard another phone being picked up, and then some kind of a click, and then a catching of breath which could have been either frightened or excited. Sounds came over the line. They were all menacing and dissonant, with an echo-chamber effect. It must have been a recording of a piece of electronic music. There was no apparent rhythm, and of course no melody, not even notes. The sounds were on another, dehumanized scale: moans of steel, and long heavy thumps, and gongs, and a rasping whine like a buzz saw, to set the teeth on edge, and finally a wail that glided higher and higher, very deliberately, like a serpent coiling itself up a tree.

Then the phone was slammed down.

We were out of touch again for a while. Finally I telephoned and the recorded voice said I'd reached a disconnected number. Had she disappeared again? Juliet would know. No, she'd only changed the number. Juliet gave me the new one. I called and got the secretary. Mrs. Ross was asleep at the moment (it was five o'clock in the afternoon), but would I care to leave a message? Oh, just say I called. Mrs. Ross didn't call back. Then was she offended by my letter? I hoped not, because it was really the mildest of criticisms, if it was even that, and I was fond of Susan and knew that in her stubborn, barricaded way she was becoming a neighbor of despair. (As I thought it over, that gesture of the electronic recording was more alarming than funny; it was as if she wanted me to hear all the agonized sounds she couldn't make herself.) I believed that Susan was fond of me, too, or rather of her image of me—"the writer," sympathetic and understanding, and of course fascinated by the character she'd drawn of herself. Yet our friendship was never quite real, more a platonic liaison with its exchanged letters, sudden appointments and secret walks.

So I did nothing and was disturbed to find how quickly I fell into thinking of Susan as someone in my past. I suppose that was a part of her character, too. In a life with so many gaps and flights and farewells, two or three months can pass and the silence is unbroken and the phone number changed yet again, and maybe she's gone forever this time because she was so seldom really here.

Ten years ago, when I first lived in California, I worked at a movie studio that was like a great neglected estate. Its back lot jumbled up places, continents and centuries under the sky. A walk through its surprises and transitions reminded me of many human lives I knew. Later the studio sold much of its land and the bulldozers came, pulverizing the Last Chance Saloon, the entrance to a Chinese temple, the façade of a turn-of-the-century mansion. A desert appeared. Then boxes of metal and glass soared upward, above patios with relentless automated fountains. Office blocks, stores, restaurants and a hotel replaced that mythical country where Tyrone Power sought the Answer in the East, and Love was a Many-Splendored Thing and Gene Tierney, in a gingerbread house, was forever a Prisoner of it.

Now most of this has gone. When you drive past the lost world, along Santa Monica Boulevard toward the ocean, you see only the fringes of another ordinary, anonymous suburb. The tall new buildings on one side, with a few giant billboards recommending Scotch and new flights to Hawaii, and on the other the grounds of a country club. Still, if you knew its past, there's a ghostliness behind the lack of charm. Going home to the beach from Beverly

Hills, I usually drive this way. Late one afternoon there is nothing around except traffic and three or four people waiting at the bus stop. One of them is a tall young man with long blond hair, barefoot, wearing faded jeans and a buckskin jacket with nothing underneath it. He thumbs a lift at me, but I can't stop because I'm in the center lane and traffic is heavy. I see his face for only a moment; a truck passes between us. I glance in the rear-view mirror and now of course his back is turned toward me. In the right lane, quite close behind, is a car driven by a chauffeur. It stops. The young man gets in. I can never tell a Pontiac from a Dodge, and maybe Susan's car is really a Ford, but it *looks* like hers and is the right color. The chauffeur is masked in a cap and dark glasses and I can only glimpse another shadowy figure in the back. I slow down, anyway, and get into the right lane as soon as possible, hoping the car will catch up and perhaps overtake me. But it turns off almost at once into a street that skirts the country-club grounds, and I've lost it.

Another month passes. Winter comes in like summer. High winds from the desert sweep everything clear. Each evening the sun goes down in a wild tropical swoon, violet and orange. Each morning sky and ocean are flawlessly blue and the horizon sharp as an ache.

A few days before Christmas the phone rings and the English secretary says, "Mrs. Ross would like to know if you can come over for a drink at five o'clock tomorrow?" Is it still the same house? Oh yes. And how is Mrs. Ross? "She's fine!" A note of surprise. "Just fine!"

Along the coast highway it still looks like summer. The ocean glitters like crystal and the day feels even warmer than it is when you hear Christmas commercials on the radio, then glance out of the car window and see the beaches packed and surfers riding the perfect waves. There are young hitchhikers everywhere, in singles and couples, some of them beautiful, others rather weird-looking. The least hopeful carry signs that read, SAN FRANCISCO. In the last year or two the hitchhiking population seems to have increased enormously, adding to the city's transience and mystery. Many travel barefoot and half naked. Survivors from the Children's Crusade must have looked like some of these. There are thousands of them, a new tribe, who get wherever they want to go without cars or money or shoes. Then, beyond Malibu, the nomads and the sense of vacation disappear, the scenes change as abruptly as on the old movie back lot, when you turned the corner from Arizona to Hong Kong. Now it's a loner's country of scattered houses, steep canyons, bare hillsides and an empty ocean. I turn off on the PRIVATE ROAD. Susan's car is parked outside the house, this time without her chauffeur at the wheel. A dead gull lies in the road and flies buzz around it. I announce myself on the telephone, the gate hums slowly open.

In the living room, a bottle of white wine waited in an ice bucket. The housekeeper said that Mrs. Ross would like me to help myself. I glanced around and saw the usual collection of magazines on the coffee table, but the silver vase on the sun deck had no flowers in it. On the couch was a book called *Sense Relaxation,* text and photographs that explained how to get to know your body by feeling and stroking and slapping it and taking a shower with your eyes closed; how to explore other people through touch and games and sharing a loaf of bread. See, experience, slow down, love. I was reading how to peel an orange when Susan came into the room.

"That's almost the best of all, I do it every day," she said immediately. "You hold the orange in your hand, smell it, then make contact with the whole thing. When you can really *feel* it, you open your eyes and *look* at it, and start peeling it very gently, watching it come apart. Then you close your eyes again and *hear* it come apart . . ." She cupped her hands, holding an imaginary orange, and it looked as if she were about to pray.

This was an image of Susan I'm unlikely to forget, the brilliant ocean a backdrop to her still figure with its cupped hands, dark hair bundled into a pony tail, eyes so intent they looked blind. She wore a very light, thin pants suit, made of crepe de Chine, I think, and the color of creamed honey. It had a delicate, hazy pattern of flowers, the palest of pinks and blues merging with each other as in an impressionist painting of dawn or twilight. As usual she wore no make-up except for the hint of eye shadow, and her skin looked paler than ever.

After a moment, her hands dropped to her sides. She gave me a reproachful look. "Now why have you been neglecting me, my friend? It's almost three months since you called."

"And since you didn't return my call."

She shook her head. "That can't be true. I'm sure I returned it."

We had a brief, meaningless argument about this, and then I said, "I thought maybe my letter offended you."

She seemed surprised. "Letter . . . ? Oh no, it was very thoughtful. Very kind. I meant to answer it."

"You did. That hideous music over the phone."

"Yes, of course!" She laughed. "I suppose I *was* a little offended."

"Why?"

"I've forgotten."

We smiled at each other. A pause occurred. She turned away, poured out a glass of wine, and I noticed her hand shook a little. She'd waited to see me, but now that I was here she seemed ill at ease. It had never been like this before.

She turned back with a rather forced smile. "So what's been happening?"

Worse and worse. This was the kind of conversation made by people who have nothing to say to each other. "I think I passed your car on Santa Monica Boulevard a few weeks ago," I said casually. "You stopped to pick up a hitchhiker."

She laughed again. "No, you couldn't have, I'm terrified of people who thumb rides. Of course, maybe my chauffeur was out running errands and *he* picked someone up . . ." A shrug, and she became preoccupied again. "Listen, I really have missed you, but I almost called and put you off. Not because I didn't want to see you, but I had another appointment—" oddly businesslike word—"which I'd forgotten about."

"That's all right, Susan. You want me to go now?"

"Not right away." Her tone implied the opposite. "At least finish your wine. We can chat for a few—"

At that moment the electronic buzz sounded. Susan looked distracted. "Dear God! Already? I hope . . ." She touched my arm. "It won't look right if you rush out the same time he comes in. So please stay for a few minutes. Please?"

Which is how I came to meet, very briefly, a man who can only be described as legendary.

There's no other word for a person who's famous but whom practically nobody has ever seen. David Almont is one of those strange heroes whose adventures are all in the physical, public world, sports and industry, but whose temperament is fearful and private. For many years he's been as withdrawn as Susan, but at the same time he's directed all kinds of business operations and made millions of dollars. In his youth (he's now in his late fifties) he was a racing-car driver and won various international championships. He was going to marry, or rumored to be having affairs with, movie stars, fashion models and beautiful women with titles acquired from divorced husbands. He bought things. An automobile plant, a shipping line, hotels in Mexico and the Caribbean, a copper mine in Nevada; but he never touched the aircraft industry because strangely enough he hated flying. He had overturned at 120 m.p.h. in a Ferrari and entered another race the next day, but being taken above the clouds was something else. He was known for reserving two or three private coaches on a coast-to-coast train, and sailing to Europe in a liner his company owned, never emerging from his five-room suite. He refused to meet the press or attend public functions, but his name was constantly in the newspapers. Apart from the deals he made, there were no facts, only speculation. Reporters wrote long non-interviews. (Was he about to acquire a casino in Las Vegas or marry a Greek princess? No . . . After a while you began to suspect that on principle he would never confirm a rumor.) He had no home, but rented a permanent bungalow at a hotel in Bel Air and a permanent penthouse at a small East Side hotel in New York. When he was thirty his hair went gray, so he never seemed to age, except in his habits, becoming more and more of a recluse, surrounded and blocked by bodyguards. The only photographs you ever saw were sneaked blurred images of a tall, lean man with a long face, usually wearing a sweater or windcheater that gave him the look of a mountaineer.

When Almont came into Susan's living room he was instantly surprised and displeased to see me. Before Susan could say anything, he gave her an accusing look. For a moment I thought he would turn around and leave at once. He was even taller than the photographs suggested, about six foot three. He wore a stained turtleneck sweater, whipcord Levis and boots. His face was tanned, with few but deep lines, a Roman nose and stern mouth. There was a star-shaped scar on his forehead, maybe from the racing-car accident. He touched it frequently. Behind him, in the front patio, a man in a dark suit appeared. He remained standing motionless, with his back to us. A moment later another bodyguard entered behind the glass of the sun deck and stood in the same way, facing the ocean.

Susan explained that I was an old and "trusted" friend, emphasizing this word, whom she'd asked to drop by. I apologized for arriving late, in order that Almont shouldn't think that Susan had wanted us to meet, and said I had to go very soon anyway. He didn't answer but looked slightly less displeased. He walked about, touching his scar, so restless that you felt standing still might actually be dangerous for him. Finally, with great reluctance, he spoke to me. It was an effort, and an unrewarding one, of course, but he was doing it for Susan's sake. In an unexpectedly light voice he asked what I did. I told him I was a writer. He looked enormously alarmed. I added that I wasn't a journalist, but wrote novels and worked in the movies.

"Oh. That kind of thing . . ." It seemed totally remote to him, but harmless, and he was relieved.

Susan said we'd known each other for a long time and I'd been a friend of Charlie's. He nodded, walked toward the sun deck and stared through the glass at the ocean. He gave no sign that he was aware of the bodyguard. I suppose I watched as if observing some new animal, trying to learn its habits; but Susan seemed to know them all. She followed him, stood quietly behind him, with an air of extraordinary attention. You could tell that she was deeply fascinated, and slightly but enjoyably frightened, and that she "understood" him. It was agreed. It was her role. He turned around suddenly, gave her a faint, tired smile and myself a sharp stare. Then he walked over to the ice bucket and picked up the bottle of wine.

"Let me get you a glass," Susan said immediately.

He shook his head, examining the label. "Is this from the case I sent you?" She gave a nod. "Goddamit!" he said. "I told them '55. The '57 is almost . . ." He broke off, slammed the bottle back in the bucket, and we felt tricked for having enjoyed it.

"It's good, though," Susan said. "Try some."

Almont shook his head again. Out of the question to drink '57. He picked up *Sense Relaxation,* held it at arm's length—so he was long-sighted—and frowned. "What's this all about?"

"I told you. It brings you back to your senses."

"Yes . . ." He frowned at the book again. "Do one for me."

Susan glanced at me, then closed her eyes. She stood very rigid, then began to relax. A smile hovered about her mouth. Almont watched her with an intent, wary expression. Her head drooped a little. She hardly breathed. Her face and hands looked ghostly white. This lasted for about a minute. Almont remained still for the first time.

"What did you hear?" he asked when she opened her eyes.

"Kettle boiling in the kitchen." The smile still hovered about Susan's mouth. "Plane somewhere above the ocean. Quite high." She picked up a cigarette. Almont took it away from her. "My wind chimes on the roof just once," she said, without a flicker of reaction. "There's only a small breeze today. The surf, of course, but that's pretty quiet today too. And one of your men has a stomach rumble. The one on the deck." She moved closer to Almont. "Somebody breathing. I think it was you. You breathe so quickly."

He stared at her, apparently spellbound. I told Susan I had to go.

"We must see each other again very soon." She made it sound unlikely. Then her eyes flickered. "Do you *have* to go now? There's plenty of food in the house. We could all—" She broke off, catching Almont's eye. "Please call me soon. I mean it."

"Of course I will."

Almont barely nodded goodby. "I'm sorry, I've just *got* to have a cigarette!" she said rather urgently. He asked how many she'd smoked today. After hesitation, she told him six. "You're a liar," he said, and handed her a cigarette with mock ceremony. She walked with me to the front door, tense again and not smiling at all. She pressed my hand, then turned away. I walked past the bodyguard in the patio and received a look of impassive contempt. Like the other on the sun deck, he was all that such men are supposed to be—husky, rat-eyed, with big hands. I looked back toward the front door. Susan was still on the threshold. She waved for me not to leave yet, and hurried over. "Mother just thought of something," she said, smiling.

Her hand rested on mine for a moment. It was icy cold. Yet she went on smiling. "Did you know that when people get lost in rain forests and jungles and difficult places like that, they always go in the wrong direction and get lost even further, because they panic? It's a fact," she said brightly. "I read it somewhere. They think they're finding their way back, but because they've blown their cool they're really getting lost forever."

The bodyguard was keeping a stony eye on us. She became aware of him. "Just rapping," she said to me, made the Peace sign and turned back to the house.

Outside the gate I saw a black Rolls with smoked-glass windows parked behind Susan's car. As I approached my own car, another guard appeared and opened the door for me. I thanked him and got no reaction. He waited until I was just inside, then slammed the door deliberately hard. Driving away, I noticed that someone had removed the dead gull and felt sure there'd be other changes. Next time I called Susan the number would be out of service again, and not even Juliet would know the new one.

Three days later, Susan and Almont were married in a private ceremony at his hotel bungalow. There were no guests, apart from the bodyguards, who also served as witnesses. For an unexplained reason a minister was flown in under escort from San Francisco. He was not available to the press.

They were reported to have left for a honeymoon, but of course no one knew where. They were reliably seen in Puerto Vallarta and Barbados. However, two days after the marriage it turned out that Almont was staying in Montreal, without Susan, making a deal to build a new hotel there.

This is how Susan noticed the rain. As usual, the storm had not been forecast. The TV weathermen said that a cold front had overtaken a warm front near San Luis Obispo, and the warm air was being lifted by cold air, which certainly meant rain somewhere, but they didn't believe any precipitation would reach Los Angeles. It began to rain heavily about ten o'clock that evening.

She had just moved into the new house. Some time before they married, Almont had bought the plateau in

Topanga Canyon. It came to about fifteen lots in all. When I met him at Susan's house I didn't know that the cabins had already been erased and the land leveled, and the ranch house was already under construction. Until it was finished, she stayed at the hotel bungalow. (I doubt that she ever left it; Almont was fanatically afraid of kidnapers.) The newspapers reported that the chain-link fence surrounding the new place was twelve feet high, and there were armed guards day and night. Until she phoned me the night before it began to rain, I'd heard nothing from her. Naturally I hadn't expected to see her—since marrying Almont she'd seen nobody, including, as she was to tell me, Almont himself—but I'd half hoped for a smuggled message of some kind. It would have been in keeping with the past. Even Juliet had heard nothing. She talked about her old friend now like the Bel Air wives after Charlie's death. ("No, she never even *mentioned* him to me. I suppose they met when she was in the Caribbean, and *pretended* she kept to herself. You know, of course, he can't cut the mustard?" I didn't. "Oh, I thought everyone knew. It's why the other women never married him, don't you see? They got so bored with expensive secret dinners and no dessert." Then why did Susan marry him? "She always liked to make things difficult for herself." And then Paul, sweetly from the chaise longue: "Hasn't your female Siddartha reached the end of her journey?") So with a nice mixture of malice and regret, Susan was struck off their list, off everybody's list.

Strangely enough, the night before Susan called I'd gone out to dinner with a friend, a painter who lived in Topanga Canyon. I left him about one o'clock in the morning and on an impulse drove a mile farther up the hill to the turn-off Susan and I had taken that day. I followed the short, steep rise to the plateau and had to brake almost immediately. Out of nowhere, it seemed, was the high mesh fence and a closed gate. Even before I stopped, floodlights were switched on and a guard ran toward me, pointing a gun. Another appeared immediately behind him. They asked what I wanted and I told them, Nothing. I used to know Mrs. Almont, I was on my way home and wanted to pass by the house. We had once taken a walk here together.

They seemed disinclined to believe me. I felt that it struck them as an impossible idea, Mrs. Almont having a friend. One of them said, "Well, now you've seen the house you can go home," and I did exactly that. As I turned around and drove away, the floodlights were switched off. In the rear-view mirror I glimpsed the outline of the house, a hundred yards or so beyond the gate. It was one-storied, in traditional ranch style. A single light came from a room at the far end. For as far as you could see, everything else was darkness.

When the rain happened next night, I was at home. The phone rang toward eleven o'clock. I picked it up and Susan's voice said immediately, "It's raining!" She made it sound like a much more extraordinary event, a tidal wave or a murder. "I was watching a movie on TV," she went on, "and in the movie it was raining, and it was quite a while before I noticed the *real* rain."

"Are you all alone up there?"

"Of course. The servants and the guards are all in their own part of the house. My bedroom's completely *separate,* you see. Was it you who came by last night?" I told her yes. "The guards said somebody came. I guessed it was you."

"A couple of years ago I was in Haiti," I said, "in Port-au-Prince, and I was driving back very late from the town to a hotel up in the hills. I took a wrong turning and found myself coming up to the back entrance of Duvalier's palace. All at once floodlights hit my car and half a dozen soldiers were swarming around me with guns. I explained I'd just lost my way, but they thought I was an assassin and searched the car. I must say, when everything was cleared up, they were much friendlier than *your* guards."

She laughed. "By the way, there's this automatic device that records all the phone conversations here." She mentioned it as a very ordinary fact. She might have been explaining there was a fireplace, or a swimming pool.

"You can't make any private calls, then?"

Another laugh. "Do you mean private or secret, my friend? There's nothing *wrong* in any call I make. As a matter of fact, when I write him tomorrow I'll tell him we spoke."

"Where is he?"

"I'm not sure. He might be in Jamaica."

"Then how will you write him?"

"I give the letter to someone who works for him. He sends it on."

I asked when she saw Almont last.

"Let's see." A pause. "Five months ago."

"Wasn't it five months ago that you married him?"

"Yes," she said after a moment. "That's right."

"Do you miss him?"

There was no answer.

"Doesn't either of you miss seeing the other?"

I heard something like a sigh. Then: "But that's not the point. And if you knew him, you wouldn't . . . At first, of course, I thought . . . But we're so incredibly alike, we're really perfect . . ." The voice trailed off. "Excuse me while I light a cigarette."

After a few seconds, she came back on the line. "Are you still there?"

"Yes. Are you, Susan?"

She laughed again. "Always and always. Oh, am I *here*!"

"But why do you never see each other?"

"We talk. And we've joined forces. Can't you see that's enough?"

"Do you ever go out?"

"I think you're getting a completely wrong idea of my life! Of course I go out!"

"Where?"

She hesitated. "Last week I went to a beautiful art show at the museum. On Monday, when it's closed. They were very kind and opened it up for us."

"Us?"

"The guards and me. And sometimes—" she made it sound like an act of extraordinary kindness—"I'm taken for a drive." Then her voice dropped to a stage whisper. "But it's better not to go out very often. It really *is* dangerous!"

"Where is the danger now, Susan?"

"I get kidnap threats. We both do." She revealed this with a tremor of excitement, followed by a little ache of satisfaction, as if the world were living up to her highest hopes. There was more than the idea of an evil tree or tower at each end of it, there were real anonymous warnings in the mail and over the phone. Voices from nowhere uttered warnings. Ominous words arrived on scraps of paper. "Before we married, he promised me I'd get them," she said. "And he's sure they'll go on forever. So it's better to stay where I am."

I asked how the days passed. She told me, very easily, there was so much to occupy her mind. She was learning French and Spanish from phonograph records, and she listened to music, and the guards had taught her to play poker. "We have our Friday-night games," she said wonderingly. "I never thought I'd enjoy anything like that, but I do." And she was reading a great deal, of course. "Are you familiar with the works of Abraham Maslow?" I said no, I'd heard of him, but didn't really know what he wrote about. "All the important things," Susan explained, "like developing your mind and your consciousness. He tells you how to reach peak experiences. That means you discipline yourself so that your mind and your senses can shift into top gear whenever you want, and you become fantastically aware and alert! I've made incredible progress in French and Spanish this way, I can chatter into a machine in both of them already, and I'm going on to German and Russian soon . . ."

In a few years, I thought, she'll have learned a dozen different languages and will be able to talk to nobody in all of them.

"Of course, living the way I do," she said, "I find I reach more peak experiences in general. It's the perfect place, up here. I've come to realize the mind can achieve *anything* so long as reality doesn't get in its way."

Then she caught her breath suddenly, and I asked what was the matter, and she murmured that she was just listening to the rain. It was falling harder now. Was it raining very hard at the beach, too? I glanced out of the window and said yes, it was coming down in torrents. Everything looked blurred and shiny and weeping.

"How beautiful. I hope it goes on and on."

"You really sound very happy."

"Of course! Are you surprised?"

"And you never feel that impatience you used to talk about?"

"No. Never anything like that. You'd be astonished if you saw me now! I am definitely one of the most patient people in the world."

"Well, I guess you have to be."

"No." She didn't catch the irony. "It's my own choice, like everything else. I'm where I always wanted to be. I'm truly free." A pause, then a faint laugh. "My only problem is, I have to watch my weight."

"How much have you gained?"

"I am not going to tell you that," she said. "And I'm going to hang up in a moment because I took a sleeping pill and it's starting to work. Did you know there are sleeping pills that stop you dreaming? Mine do. I'm glad, because I never liked my dreams . . ." I heard a long yawn, and when she spoke again her voice became gradually fainter, losing itself slowly in the sound of the rain. "In a way I wish you were here . . . And yet I don't . . . I'd love to see you but I don't *need* anyone any . . . So good being alone in this house—*basically* alone, you know what I mean?—up here, so safe, in the rain . . ."

"Susan."

No answer.

"Susan?"

"Excuse me. I think I actually dropped off for a moment."

"Will I ever see you again?"

There was another yawn. "It doesn't seem likely, I'm afraid." Then I thought I heard her laughing very softly.

"Are you laughing again?"

"Yes, I suppose so."

"Why?"

"I just thought of something. Mother once tried to end her life! Can you imagine? There was a time I was actually crazy enough to try a thing like that." And then, suddenly: "Well, goodby!" she said and put down the phone.

So, with a click like a wire being cut, her number is finally disconnected.

GARY CARSON

East of Hollywood you reach a dead, flat no man's land. The surrounding hills are far away and often masked in smog. Geologically, the rock strata have dipped down to a wide, level expanse here, and decay has slid into the section too. Paint peels on the jumble of buildings. Neon signs have a letter or two missing. Sidewalks betray ancient cracks and the smog has left a layer of grime upon everything, faces included. The boulevards are lined with seedy delicatessens, tailors' shops, used-car lots, hamburger and taco stalls, For Rent notices, builders' warehouses, corner bars, eccentric porticoes bearing only mysterious initials, H.I.O. and M.U.N. Above them, fashionable ladies on billboards recommend one to cook with gas or drink a particular brand of vodka. People walk along the streets with a lost, gray air, as if no one has told them the set was struck many years ago. The day *seems* to end a little sooner here, and the first lights come on a little earlier.

In an area not zoned for living, Loney Pardoe lives in a converted warehouse with OTT PENCIL CO. painted in fading black letters on its side wall. You climb a dark, steep flight of wooden steps and find yourself in a loft. Its main section is surrounded by stained white walls and a high, shadowy ceiling. It contains an old tufted sofa and some basket chairs, a long dining table with stools placed around it, scatter rugs on an olive linoleum floor, and against one wall, not really hidden by a rattan screen, a kitchen sink, greenish refrigerator and antique stove. Corridors lead off in various directions. They turn past several small rooms and alcoves containing only box-spring beds with drab, rumpled Madras cotton covers and gray pillow cases. Somewhere is a bathroom the size of a toilet on a plane. It has a mottled, grumbling W.C., a washbowl with a single dripping faucet, a streaked and rickety little tub. Finally, if you don't lose your way, you arrive at Loney's studio. This is an area almost without daylight. Loney decorates wooden blocks with the faces of Greek gods, makes collages from old shirts and towels, aluminum foil, beads and photographs, and paints over store dummies, replacing a nipple with a pair of smiling lips and a row of bright teeth, putting an extra eye in the navel.

Loney's art, however, is only a hobby. Having been left a little money by his parents, he can devote himself to his main work, which is sheltering young wanderers and fugitives. A few of them are wanted by the police, most have simply run away from family or the whole world outside. There are usually eight or ten people sleeping around the loft. Loney sometimes forgets exactly who is there. A stranger rises suddenly from an alcove bed, Loney fixes him with pale, astonished eyes, his babyish, fortyish face lights up and he says, "Oh, what a nice surprise! Now who *are* you?" They all seem to sleep a great deal. One or two may work at night, washing dishes at restaurants or checking in clients at steam baths; the others just like to sleep all day, anyway. Loney cooks for them and takes their dirty clothes to a laundromat. "My only hang-up," he admits, "is cleanliness." His transients are his cause, although he's not the kind of person you associate with a cause, and much too innocent and practical to claim that he has one. "They just need me" is as far as he will go. Or, perhaps: "It's such a *bitch* of a time. Somebody has to do something." He is particularly sympathetic to draft dodgers—"a very beautiful and important profession"—and Negroes so long as they're not terrorists—"I can't have any violence around my little place, it's not fair to the others, and besides I just don't like it, it's bad news"—and boys and girls who run away from plastic middle-class homes—" Doesn't there have to be a halfway house between Haight-Ashbury and summer camp?" Apart from cleanliness and peacefulness, there's only one other house rule: no hard drugs. "Grass is a groove, of course, though myself I'll take a Black Russian usually, but needles and reds—I'm not a hospital, you see, just a refuge."

Nothing is expected of guests in return. Loney makes overtures, never demands. Attracted to someone, he might ask casually, "Do you think it would be cool if we went to bed together?" If the boy says yes, Loney is overwhelmed with delight—"Oh, I'm *so* happy!" If the answer is no, he shrugs and gives a reassuring smile. "That's perfectly cool too, just thought I'd ask!"

Ask any of them about Loney and they all use the same word: "Beautiful."

He invited me to dinner about a month after Susan married Almont. There were two others in the loft when

I arrived. One was a young Negro who'd given up professional football to write poetry. He lay on a bed in an alcove leading directly off the loft, wearing only a pair of orange jockey shorts, dead roach in his mouth, and said the images were coming. The other was a beautiful, intense girl who called herself Magnette. She worked part time in a vegetarian restaurant and acted in a little-theater group. She believed improvisation was the only valid dramatic form. The actor could no longer submit himself to the tyranny of a writer's words, especially if the language was antiquated, like Shakespeare's. Her group took a situation and *grew* with it. Acting had to be a way of finding out about yourself. Later her boyfriend arrived wearing only a pair of jeans and carrying a phonograph album. She gave me a sweet smile and disappeared with him to a room at the back. They listened to Blood, Sweat and Tears until it was time for dinner.

Steam was pouring out of a Mexican casserole on the ancient stove, drenching the room with vegetable perfume, when two more arrived. A boy, his long dark curly hair tied up with a piece of string, sold copies of the Los Angeles *Free Press* on the street and was studying to be an astrologer. A small, fair-haired, childlike girl, who told me in a tiny voice that she'd been married for six months to a doctor, was using all her alimony on flying lessons. She said that her ambition was to pilot a Lear jet upside down above the ocean, completely stoned. It must be the most fantastic sensation in the world. She had a little portable radio that picked up all the flight signals from the airport and listened to it with a lovely, shy concentration, spellbound by news from the sky.

Loney fluttered calmly around them all. They were his charming, promising children talking about what they wanted to be when they grew up, and in the meantime he encouraged them to eat their dinner. Fiercely loyal, he whispered in my ear that Magnette was a beautiful actress, the footballer had written beautiful things, better than Rod McKuen, the little aviatress would one day break records, and the boy who sold the *Free Press* was so perceptive he could guess your astrological sign right after having met you. I asked the boy what sign he thought I was. "Oh, you're Aries," he said at once. I shook my head and told him Leo. He gave me a completely unperturbed look. "Then you've got Aries rising." I admitted this was true. "Of course it's true," he said. "I got strong Aries vibrations the moment I met you, and honestly I'm never wrong." Then he patted my arm. "I guess you know your age is ending? Don't worry. Aquarius is going to be great for everyone." The aviatress suddenly pulled back her headset and gave an ecstatic smile. "Wow! A plane's just coming in from *Peru*!"

Footsteps occurred on the stairs. A very tall, astonishingly handsome young man entered, wearing a fringed buckskin jacket, bleached Levis and desert boots. He had blond hair falling to his shoulders, a black leather headband, and eyes blue as the night sky. There was a Viking air about him, something of the pirate and the hunter. You could tell that he was, so to speak, the star boarder. Loney ran up to him enthusiastically, said there was plenty of food left, and pointed to a stool. He sat down beside me. Loney introduced us. His name was Gary Carson. He looked at me very steadily, with a kind of ironic penetration, then began to eat. I knew at once that his face was familiar, but couldn't remember for a minute or two where I'd seen him before. Then, in my mind's eye, I superimposed him on a different setting: Santa Monica Boulevard, lines of traffic, a bus stop in the late-afternoon sun. A blond hitchhiker thumbed a ride and a car I thought was Susan's pulled up.

From the first, I believe, he sensed a link between us. Several times during dinner he gave me the same quick, scrutinizing look. When I said something, he answered noncommittally and turned away—not to dismiss me, but as if for some reason I made him unsure of his ground. Then he excused himself to go to the bathroom. Loney perched on his stool and said in my ear, "I'll paint you a quick picture. Gary's been dodging the draft for more than two years. He went south of the border with some chick, then he met the captain of a Japanese freighter who's smuggled him into Japan and back a couple of times. Since he came back this time another chick's been keeping him, but he got bored. You can imagine, looking the way he does, he gets plenty of offers. I met him last week in an all-night movie." A sigh. "He plays very hard to get."

Later in the evening, the group began to break up. The footballer returned to his alcove bed and dozed. Loney and the young astrologer went off somewhere in the back. Magnette and her boyfriend also disappeared, and you could hear them playing more records. The aviatress sat in a corner with her radio. In front of my chair, Gary suddenly squatted on his knees. "You're a writer. Tell me what to do."

It was more a command than a plea. His eyes rested on my face, still with an irony somewhere in their depths.

"I reported for the draft," he said, "like they told me to. I played it as far out as I could but they classified me A-one and ordered me to report back in a few days. I thought, Shit, I don't want to fight in any stupid war. On the other hand, I'm not a pacifist."

"How is that?"

"Well, you know. If you're a pacifist, you have to join the club. Like belonging to a church or a political party, something dumb like that. You're not yourself any more. The cause of going to war is so lousy and rotten, it shouldn't even *be* a cause. So I wasn't going to lose my identity by joining the cause of *not* going to war. So I just didn't report back. A girl took me to Mexico with her. We stayed there a couple of months, then drove back across the border one night. No problem. Since then I've kept moving around. There's this friend who gets me in and out of Japan."

"Do you worry a lot about being caught?"

He shook his head. "The longer you get away with it, the less likely they'll ever catch you. I'm pretty confident I can get by forever, somehow."

"Then what's your problem?"

"There's no future in it. As long as I'm outside the law, I can't settle down and *do* anything."

"What do you want to do?"

He grinned. "I don't know yet. D'you have a cigarette?" I gave him one. "Match?" The tone was almost peremptory. "I just want to get in a situation that doesn't pressure me. Of course I *could* get myself off the hook—" he snapped his fingers—"like that! My father's a brigadier general, one Silver Star, hot stuff, knew all the in places like World War

II and Korea. If I went back with my tail between my legs and agreed to join up after all, he could swing it."

"I'm sure you don't want to do that."

"Right. Anything that involves my father is something I don't want to do. Besides, *if* I did it, it would mean these last two years were completely wasted." He looked suddenly disconsolate. "Or maybe they're wasted anyway."

I smiled. "You're pretty good at convincing yourself the situation is impossible from every point of view."

"I don't like that remark." His voice was sharp. "*I* don't convince myself. Society convinces me, or tries to. It refuses to leave people alone." His eyes rested on me again, very dark. "So you don't have any suggestion at all?"

"People like you have started new lives in Canada."

"Thanks a lot."

"Maybe if you hang on a little longer, the war will be over and there'll be some kind of amnesty."

"In this country?" He gave me a pitying look. "That'll be the day. Amnesty means forgiving. The last thing they forgive you here is shitting on their rotten flag. You've got to *bleed* on it."

"If your father pulled strings, could you go back and somehow get yourself classified unfit? Emotionally unstable, or whatever they call it?"

Gary laughed. "They'd be so out to get me this time around, I could cut off my leg or tell them I screwed little boys, they'd still airmail me out to die in some lousy swamp."

"Do you want me to say there's no way out?"

"Maybe." He nodded rather grimly. "Anyway, I appreciate your lack of sympathy. It's a kick. I really mean that."

He punched my leg. "And I guess I deserve it. What's so special about my whole deal? Isn't everybody in some kind of a hopeless bag? Isn't all they can hope for to move around a bit inside it?" Then he smiled. "Now I'm going to ask for sympathy. Don't you consider that statement I just made a pretty sad philosophy for someone like me?"

About a week later, late in the afternoon, my phone rang. "This is Gary Carson," his voice said. "Do you remember me?"

"Yes, I remember you."

"Well, I seem to be pretty close to your house. I'm calling from that service station down in the canyon. Are you very busy or can I drop by and see you?"

In less than two minutes he arrived in an old Volkswagen convertible. He looked rather elegant this time, wearing a biscuit-colored fisherman's knit sweater with a crew neck, and tight corduroy pants of the same shade. Also, he'd cut his hair—not drastically, just to unisex length. The deep red paint of the Volkswagen was worn here and there and had a few bronze splotches, but it was immaculately clean and polished. "The color's turning very groovy," he said. "Like an old villa in Italy."

"You've found time in your short life to go to Italy as well as Japan?"

"Oh, I've been all over Europe." He sounded surprised that I should be surprised. "I went there from Japan, the first time. I made Paris and the south of France and Venice and Florence and Rome. Beautiful!" For a moment his eyes clouded over. Then he glanced out of the windows of my living room, toward the canyon and the ocean. "I like your house." His mouth twitched with a faint smile. "Do a lot of people tell you it reminds them of the south of France?" I nodded. "They're wrong. The colors are all different. And the light, too. But I can see why you live here. It's the next best thing."

"Gary, how old are you?"

"Twenty-one." He grinned. "The age of consent. Do you have a cigarette?"

I gave him one. This time, without saying anything, he merely waited for me to light it. Then he sat down in a chair facing the windows, gazed at the ocean again, gave a contented sigh. I asked if he'd like a drink.

"That's what I call friendly." He lay back, stretched out his legs. "I've been off the hard stuff for a while, but I think I'll have a Scotch now. No water. Just rocks." When I brought him the drink, he asked, "How long have you known Loney?"

"For years. He was one of the first people I met when I came to California."

"Oh. Of course. You're English." He smiled. "Crazy of me to forget, considering your accent. Your health, sir!" As he drank, he watched me above the rim of the glass. "You like Loney?"

"Very much."

"Yes, he has a good heart." Gary frowned. "But you can't stay there too long."

"No?"

"No." He shook his head emphatically. "It's depressing. You begin to feel you're part of some underground freak show. The bag closes too tight."

"All the same, you're lucky he took you in."

There was a pause. When he answered, his voice sounded hard and remote. "I *was* lucky."

I stared at him. "I can't believe he threw you out. Loney would never throw anyone out—unless they did something really violent, or vicious." Gary's mouth twitched with the same faint smile. "You're not violent or vicious," I said.

"Right." He frowned again. "But someone in Italy called me *cattivo*. And somebody else in France thought I was *méchant*." He pronounced both words impeccably. "They were joking, of course. I just put that remark about Loney in the past because I think of him that way now." He took another sip of his drink, eyes very alert above the rim of the glass. "I can't continue to think of Loney in the present."

"What's the alternative?"

"Who knows?" He didn't sound very interested. "By the way, are you busy later? I hope not, because I'd love to have dinner with you."

I took him to a place at the beach, with a picture window overlooking the ocean. Lights winked along the coast in the clear, crisp night. As we sat down, he glanced around at the other diners. "My God, California's middle class. Almost everyone's drunk, Martini drunk or Scotch drunk. How about some white wine? It's the only cool thing to drink when you're by the ocean."

"I've got something to ask you," I said.

"*Super!*" His accent was deliberately mock-British. "I want you to ask me things."

"How did you find my house so quickly? It's not easy."

The question seemed to disappoint him. "No problem. Loney gave me your address and I looked up the street on the map. I always do that." He sounded very businesslike, matter-of-fact. "Wherever I go, I get a map of where I am. I have a fantastic sense of direction and I can always find my way. So long as I've got a map." The waiter brought our wine. Gary insisted on being the taster. He sniffed, took a sip. His face was expressionless. He twisted the bottle toward himself and read the label. It was a California brand. Finally he said: *"Vin du pays."*

"You approve?"

"Of course. I'd expect you to know about wine, anyway." Then he laughed. "Have you guessed I don't speak French? Or Italian? Just a few rather groovy phrases, not the usual guidebook stuff of what time does the next train leave?' and 'please send for the doctor immediately,' but *méchant* and *vin du pays* and *con* and of course *voulez-vous danser avec moi?* Now, ask me something more interesting."

I said nothing at all, and he grimaced. "Not interested?" I shook my head. "Let's not make a big thing of it," I said. "I'll ask you a few things as time goes by."

"Okay." He drained his wine, poured out some more. "I didn't mean to push too hard. My insecurity must be showing. I'm really fantastically insecure."

I smiled. "Yes, I can see that."

His face went suddenly hard. "I've never read any of your books, but if you don't believe what I just said, they can't be much good, because you're not very perceptive."

"So tell me why you're insecure."

A couple sat down at the booth next to us. The girl stared at Gary with frank approval. His eyes flickered.

"Did you see that? It answers your question. I mean, a lot of people look at me that way, and of course I know why, and of course it's a groove to turn people on. But I hate the idea that my face is my fortune. It's pretty insulting to the rest of me."

"Yes," I said lightly. "It's hard to be beautiful."

He kicked me under the table. "You don't take me seriously yet, but you will. Now, this girl I went to Mexico with, to avoid the draft—let me tell you something she said down there." He lowered his voice and leaned across the table, his face almost touching mine. "'I'd like to walk down the street with you,' she said, 'holding your cock in my hand, just to let everyone know how beautiful it is.' Well . . ." He leaned back again, frowning. "That's what broke us up, really. I thought, Jesus, all she wants is to show off my cock in public. Big deal. Pretty insulting." He looked at me, expecting commiseration. "Women do things like that. They get this image of you as a fantastic lover and you have to live up to it. What a bore." Then he laughed. "I'm lying again. Kind of, anyway. What *really* broke us up was—I started smoking a lot of hash down there, and I couldn't get it together enough to keep her happy."

Involuntarily, I looked at Gary's eyes. He noticed this at once. "Yes," he said quietly. "You're right. You can look deep into them and tell."

"That you're a liar or a hophead?"

He smiled, blinked, glanced away, then looked back at me, unsmiling. His eyes were not only a very dark shade of blue, but deeply set. You thought of entrances to caves. When you isolated Gary's eyes from the rest of his face, there was a curious deadness about them. They were beautiful and somehow not quite human. They didn't light up when he smiled. I couldn't imagine them with tears, only how they looked when he was stoned—like pieces of smoked glass, or of dark transparent plastic with no light on it.

"But that's all over," he said. "The hash bit. When they made it another stupid cause, I got out."

The waiter brought the check and laid it tactfully on the table between us. Gary pushed it over to me without a word. I took out an American Express card and he remarked: "So you've fallen victim to our credit system." I asked if he disapproved of it. "I'm in no position to approve or disapprove. But just imagine this. A day comes when the government passes a new law. Everybody has to pay at once for what he wants. Nothing in the world is deferred any more. That's a kicky idea, kind of closing the time gap between desire and what it costs you."

"But the best things in life are free."

"Wow. You're even deeper than me." He smiled and pocketed my cigarettes. I drove him back to my house and he didn't get out of the car at once. He lay back in the seat and closed his eyes. The night was very clear and still. There was a full moon; its light caught his face. It looked extraordinarily calm and white and young. In the distance I could hear surf breaking.

"Well," he said and rested his arm on the back of my seat. It stayed there for a few seconds, then he gave a restless sigh and opened the door. He walked over to his Volkswagen and leaned against it, watching me. I asked if he wanted to come in for a drink. "No, not really." He paused, motionless, still watching me, his face still blanched in the moonlight, like a carving on the prow of a ship. "But I'd like to come in if I'm invited to stay the night."

"You really don't want to go back to Loney's?" I said.

He shook his head. "I've had that scene. Even if you say no, I won't go back."

"Then you'd better come in."

He still didn't move. "I'm glad I was right about you."

"In what way?"

"That you're the kind of person I can ask a thing like that." He opened the door of his Volkswagen and took out a large suitcase.

"I see you came prepared for this moment."

He tapped the case. "Everything I have in the world." He followed me into the house in silence. As I closed the front door, he said in a rather sharp, bargaining way: "Just one night."

In the small hours we lay smoking in bed together, and I laughed suddenly. "I've got another question for you now. And I think it's interesting. In your opinion, who seduced who—or whom?"

"That's easy. *I* am never seduced." He turned his head away and blew a long smoke ring into the room. Then, with a switch of mood that seemed to me typical, although I didn't know him well, he said: "Got any ice cream in the house?"

I shook my head.

"I've got a real thing coming on for ice cream. Let's go out and get some." He jumped out of bed, began putting on clothes. I didn't move and looked unenthusiastic. "Oh, come *on*!" he said. "You've got to do this with me."

He was proposing a ritual. If I turned it down, I would somehow spoil everything that had happened. "Do you often do this?" I asked as I got out of bed.

"What?"

"Have a desire for ice cream after sex."

He seemed surprised. "I don't know, I never thought about it." He slipped on his sweater. "I suppose maybe I do. Think it's too weird?"

"No. But it's new."

"Different people want all sorts of crazy different things after making it. I once knew a girl who had to have french fries."

"For Christ's sake. That would really turn me off."

"Well, you're a romantic." Then he looked thoughtful. "I always assumed I knew what I was doing and was pretty aware of myself. Now you've brought up something about me I never realized before. I go for ice cream after sex."

On the whole, the discovery appeared to please him. We went outside and he wanted to drive me in his Volkswagen. It was about three o'clock and very chilly, a sickle moon circled by haze low over the ocean. The streets were deserted; almost every window in every house was dark. I began to feel an enjoyable atmosphere of conspiracy; we were like dreadful addicts on our way to a desperate fix.

The all-night coffee shop in Santa Monica was sprinkled with its usual customers, all looking like extras on a movie set. Two men in overalls sat at the counter, smoking. A man and a woman, together yet alone at a booth in the corner, sullenly munched hamburgers. A sad-looking girl with long untidy hair flicked through a copy of the *Free Press*. You could tell she was consulting the Personal ads.

(What was she after? A threesome in the San Fernando Valley? A quiet sensitive w/m who needed bringing out? Or just a well-built guy who guaranteed satisfaction?) The waitress came to take our order and Gary asked what kind of ice cream she had. "Strawberry or vanilla or the house sundae." He asked what the sundae was like. "Ice cream, chopped nuts, maraschino cherry, whipped cream, coconut, hot fudge sauce." He ordered two. I told him I couldn't possibly eat such a thing, and he looked disapproving. "We must have the same," he said.

While we waited, the girl suddenly got up. Carrying the *Free Press,* she went to the pay phone and dialed a number. Obviously her case was urgent, but who could she be calling in the middle of the night? "Not a masseur," Gary said. "Only guys do that. Girls settle for one of those vibrators." A personable refined male, I suggested, needing love Any Time? He shook his head. "I think she found a message for *her.* You know, 'Linda I love you, call me, Tom.'" He grinned. "Believe it or not, some crazy girl actually placed an ad like that for *me* a couple of months ago." I wondered if he'd answered it. "Are you kidding? People who do that kind of thing are strictly sick."

Whoever the girl was calling didn't answer. She walked slowly, sadly back to her table, unaware that the answer might be at hand, for one of the men in overalls was watching her intently.

The sundaes arrived, looking much too real. They were like soft sculpture, one of Dali's wrist watches made of cheese. Gary ate ravenously. I took one spoonful and was overwhelmed by the sweet chemical taste. However, the fact that I swallowed any at all seemed to satisfy him. We had, so to speak, slit our flesh and mingled our blood, and the pact was sealed.

Leaving the coffee shop, we got into his car. He drove down to the ocean without saying a word and parked on a lot overlooking the beach. The surf was very quiet; the haze still circled the moon. We leaned over the railings and looked down. Gary put his arm around my neck. Another night scene was occurring below, one or two shadowy figures walking by themselves along the sand. "Silly bastards," Gary said. "It's risky to begin with, and besides, anyone you met here would have to be a creep."

Back home, he took off his clothes, got into bed, gave an enormous yawn, said "Goodnight" and fell asleep at once.

I awoke with a start. The blinds were still drawn but sunlight filtered through them. A young bird peeped outside. Gary sat on the edge of the bed, wearing my bathrobe. I received his ironic look. "Good morning," he said. "What was your first thought when you woke up and saw me here?"

"It's too early for that kind of thing."

"Pull yourself together."

"Surprise," I said. "Wondering who in hell is that person, and then remembering."

"What kind of surprise? Pleasant or unpleasant?"

"Oh, pleasant," I said.

"It never occurred to you that you're a different person this morning?" I stared at him. His mouth twitched faintly. "You're a criminal," he said. "Harboring a wanted man, a coward who shits on his country's flag. How do you feel now?"

"Fine."

He moved away. I noticed his suitcase on the floor, open and half unpacked. He picked up a suit on a hanger. "My only one, but at least it's Cardin. When you travel around with everything in one case, you don't have many changes to ring, so each one better be good. Besides my Cardin I've got the sweater and pants I wore yesterday, and a Brioni jacket, and my Western stuff, and a spare pair of Levis. Plus one pair each of boots, Gucci shoes, sneakers. Plus a dress shirt and two other groovy ones." He showed me a brilliant flowered shirt, then a white Mexican blouse with ruffled sleeves. "And that's it. But it covers just about every occasion. By the way, I've made coffee."

After a moment, I said, "I get the impression you're making plans to stay more than one night."

He hung the suit in the clothes closet. "Will I be in your way if I do?"

"No. I'm glad you're staying."

"Don't be too glad." He walked slowly back toward me and sat on the edge of the bed again. "There's no one special in your life right now, right?"

I nodded.

"Why is that?"

I said, "No reason. There just doesn't happen to be."

"Wish there were?"

"Sometimes."

"Hmmm!" he said. "You don't *really* wish, because if you did, there would be."

I said that he was probably right.

"I know it. You're basically a loner, like me. That's why . . ." He broke off suddenly, moved away again. He stood in the middle of the room as if uncertain what to do. Then he pulled up a blind. I turned on my side, away from the window.

"Go on," I said.

I heard another blind pulled up, then his voice. "That's why I won't get in your way and you won't get in mine. Okay?"

"Oh, beautiful," I said.

"I guess you've got to write or something today, so I'm going down to the beach. It's starting to be a fantastic day. I'll be back around four o'clock, but just in case—" a quick hesitation—"something comes up, could I have a key?" I told him where to find a spare one. "See you later, then." His hand pressed my shoulder. I looked up and saw him dressed in Levis and a tank-top. "Don't forget, coffee's made." He waved, then started to leave. In the doorway he paused. "I really am quite glad I met you," he said, sounding more surprised than happy. He began another false exit. "By the way, on top of the other stuff in my case are all the love letters I've ever received. I was going over them this morning while you were still asleep. Read them if you like." Another wave and he was gone. I heard the front door slam, then his voice calling up from the patio below. "Have a good day now!" A moment later his car started, and he drove away.

His suitcase stood in the middle of the room, still only partially unpacked. I noticed a small portable tape recorder, some cassettes, a pair of silver cuff links elegantly set with sapphires, paperback editions of *The Razors Edge, Siddartha* and *The Dharma Bums,* and a U.S. passport. Opening this, I saw Gary's photograph but a different name—Lawrence Ryder. To my eyes it was perfectly faked and must have been done by a professional. He had traveled last year in France, Italy, Morocco. There was also a tourist card, issued two years ago in Mexico City but unused, for Costa Rica.

The love letters were not exactly that. Kept neatly in their envelopes and packaged together with a rubber band, they were notes from about thirty different people, all over the last two years. He'd apparently had brief affairs with most of them; the rest made offers. The letters from those who wanted him but, on the evidence of what was written, hadn't had him, were passionate almost to the point of despair. The letters from ex-lovers were casual and friendly, hoping that things were all right, hoping vaguely to see him again sometime, but none expressed real regret that the affair was over. They came from a French girl at the Sorbonne, another who was a model, the male secretary of an Italian industrialist, the wife of the same industrialist, a movie actress in Rome who'd had a walk-on in a Fellini film, a girl once quite well known in Hollywood movies and now married to an English producer, from whom there was also a letter. Gary had apparently spent a month with the wife in St. Tropez and ten days with the husband in Tangier. (In the same way, a week with the secretary on Capri, two weeks with the industrialist's wife at Ischia.) A German offered to pay Gary's passage to San José and let him stay at his house there. This explained the tourist card; presumably Gary thought of accepting but changed his mind. I felt glad something better had come up. The letter was full of promises that would clearly never be kept:

"I offer you my heart and your freedom," "It has always been in my nature to give more than I receive," and so on. An American, about to move on from the Gritti in Venice to the Grand Hotel du Cap Ferrat, affectionately brushed Gary off. "I hesitate to offer advice to such an exceptionally charming and intelligent young man. But anyone over forty is not necessarily a patsy." He was a Harvard professor taking a sabbatical to write a book and, judging from the hotel addresses, must have had private means. A strange letter from Copenhagen was signed "Melinda." From various remarks—"What a pity our timing was so bad" and "You came into my life at the one time I wasn't ready for anyone" and a reference to a doctor—I decided she was a transsexual. Finally, there was the ad cut out from the *Free Press*. "Larry R. please call Sally O."

Some of the letters were addressed to Gary in Europe, mainly at hotels, others to different places in the U.S., a house in New Orleans, a ranch in Arizona, Loney's P.O. box number. All began "Dear Gary," but the name on the envelope was always Lawrence Ryder. For a moment it struck me as unexpectedly naïve of him to have admitted his situation to everybody. Then I remembered that he was, after all, only twenty-one.

He returned a few minutes after four o'clock. I was at my desk, working on a movie script, unaware of his presence until he spoke. Walking around barefoot is very good for making surprise entrances.

"Nothing came up. But I didn't really want it to. Let's have a drink."

"It's too early. Besides, I want to finish something."

Instead of answering, he stood close behind my chair and began massaging my neck and shoulders. It made me smile. "Feels good, doesn't it?" It did, but this wasn't the reason I smiled. The gesture struck me as a sly yet innocent attempt at imposing his will. All the same, it succeeded. I told Gary to make himself a drink, because I didn't want one yet, and we went to the living room. He settled in the same chair, facing the windows. As I'd done last evening, I sat on the couch. He grinned. I realized that without thinking I'd conformed to the pattern he chose, and he'd noticed it at once. The first habit in a relationship had been established, sitting together like this at the end of a day.

It occurred to me that Gary declared his own freedom and then began to create little, imprisoning, domestic rituals. I felt mildly annoyed. In the past, many others must have done exactly what I'd just done, and for the same reason. It was difficult not to do what Gary wanted even when he so obviously took it for granted that you would.

"Nothing really came up," he said. "But I met a lot of people."

"What kind of people?"

"Winter ones. A beach in summer is kind of awful, much too crowded, and if there's anyone worthwhile to latch on to, you never get to find them. But on a beautiful day in winter, it's different. It's not vacation time, so they shouldn't be there at all unless they're like me. On the move. Just somewhere in the world. I met some kids trying to get themselves together into a rock group, then I played volleyball with some exercise freaks, then I talked to a girl who said I ought to be an actor and her father was a producer. She invited me to dinner tonight, but I decided against it."

"Why?"

"Well, first of all her old man is only in TV, and then I could tell she's the type who makes it a big deal—sex, getting involved, you owe me everything. Did you read those letters?" I nodded. "The ones that promised me the whole shooting match—she was like that." Sidelong glances were not at all in Gary's line, but now he gave me a look that wasn't quite direct. "What did you think of the letters?"

"You certainly get around." I paused. "But why do you always tell people that you've got a false passport and you're dodging the draft? Isn't that pretty risky?"

Gary shrugged. "Not if you're lucky. And you're always lucky if you believe in luck."

"You can push it too far."

"I don't think so." His voice was serious. "Anyway, if I'm going to say yes to someone, I can't be Lawrence Ryder the night before and then admit I've got problems, I'm really Gary Carson, in the morning. It's not right. Of course, if I decide I've got to get away from someone, they're spooking me and might turn nasty, I clear out in the middle of the night. But I always write a letter afterwards—" he gave me a straight, virtuous look—"making some excuse and telling them how great it all was." Then his face clouded over. "Of course," he began, "it's . . ." and broke off.

"Go on."

"Nothing." He gazed out of the window. "Look, there's a hummingbird out there. You've got everything."

"Were you going to say there are times when having to move on, and all that, gets to be a drag?"

He shrugged. "Maybe. I'm not quite sure what I was going to say."

"The first time we met, you told me what worried you about your situation was—"

"Nothing *worries* me," he interrupted sharply. "I never said anything like that. There's just one aspect of my life that's not completely satisfying."

"The temporary aspect?"

"That's the word." For an instant he looked almost melancholy, hunching himself in the chair. "That's the word for everything."

The sun was going. We both listened to the distant sound of surf. Then an ambulance siren whined somewhere along the coast highway. "About a couple of months ago," I said, "I saw you on Santa Monica Boulevard, thumbing a ride."

He grinned, totally cheerful again. "You did? Why in hell didn't you pick me up?"

"I was in the center lane and there was too much traffic. But I saw another car stop for you."

"So I got there," Gary said. "Wherever it was, I got there again." He thought it over. "I thumbed a lot of rides before someone gave me my Volkswagen."

"Do you know the name Susan Ross?"

He looked blank, then shook his head.

"The car was driven by a chauffeur. If it belonged to whom I think it did, there was a beautiful dark-haired woman in her late thirties sitting in the back."

He stared at me. He grimaced suddenly and beat the side of his head with his fist. "Oh *no*! She's a friend of yours?" And then, before I could answer: "In her *late* thirties?"

I nodded. "Thirty-nine, I think."

"You're putting me on." He looked astonished. "But she didn't seem . . . *Thirty-nine?*" he repeated, between disbelief and awe. "I've never gone for a woman that old."

"Why does age only matter to you with women?"

"I don't know. I never thought about it. Why do you keep turning up crazy things about me? First the ice-cream bit and now . . . Think it's too weird?"

"No. Rather nice and sentimental."

"Sentimental?" It alarmed him. "How do you work that out?"

"You seem to think there's something specially sad and difficult about a woman getting older."

"Well, a man can handle it. He can even get more attractive with it." He became almost melancholy again. "Though it must be sad and difficult for anyone getting old . . ." The shadow passed swiftly. He grinned at me. "Sorry. Old*er.* Will you see forty again, by the way?"

"No."

"Does it bug you?"

"I haven't flipped."

"There you go, proving my point. This Susan was almost out of her mind. Thirty-nine," he said again. "So she's a friend of yours?"

"I used to see her quite often. Then she married David Almont."

Gary looked blank. "Who's that?"

"You never heard of him?" I was pleased to find that his precocity was not, after all, unlimited. "They call him a legend. One of the ten richest men in the world."

"Old? An old man?"

"Late fifties."

"You can't tell me *that's* not old. So why did she marry him? She's pretty rich herself, isn't she?"

"Yes. But tell me what happened."

At that time, Gary said, he was one of a group living in a large unfurnished house in the Hollywood hills. The owner, moving to New York and unable to sell it, had lent it to a friend who invited several of his friends to share it. They included a girl with an illegitimate child, a middle-aged hippie trying to raise money to finish an underground movie, a struggling actor. They all slept on mattresses on the floor. Rats scuttled across the attic every night. Gary had been depressed for a few weeks and began smoking a good deal of grass. His life seemed more temporary than usual, he was broke, and one day a prospective buyer came to look at the house. "I had a couple of possibilities left, but I wasn't crazy about either of them." The actor told him about a movie director who lived in Malibu and was looking for a houseboy. "I needed a change and thought it might be groovy for a month or two. Just the idea of getting a job was pretty far out, and if I didn't like it I could always walk." He telephoned the director, who asked him to come out for an interview. Since there was no one who could drive him out to the beach that day, he had to hitch a ride. The first driver who picked him up was only going as far as the Beverly Hilton Hotel and dropped him near the bus stop. He waited for about fifteen minutes, then a car driven by a chauffeur pulled up for him. A woman sat alone in the back. Her face was almost entirely screened by a broad-brimmed hat and dark glasses. She asked where he was going, and it turned out that she lived a few miles beyond the director's house and could take him right to the door. She said that she'd met the director, and Gary explained about the job, and she seemed somehow disturbed. A silence fell. He asked if she thought the job a bad idea, and she said, "Not if that's what you want."

By this time Gary had decided that he liked her. He could hardly see her face and she seemed nervous and strange, but he was getting interesting vibrations. He began telling her about himself. She was extremely sympathetic. "That's one thing about telling them—you kind of place yourself in their hands and it's flattering, they go for it." Soon they were talking about the state of the world. Susan explained that she too, in her own way, found it a difficult place in which to live. "I could tell she meant it. My only problem was, I couldn't really find out what *her* problem was. But now I know she's thirty-nine . . ." At one point, Susan remarked, "Did you know that they have the same word in Tibet for 'beautiful' and 'happy'?" Gary shook his head, and she sighed. "But only in Tibet," she said.

He mentioned that he'd been reading *Siddartha,* and she became animated and asked his opinion of Jung. "I never read him," Gary told her, "but I always heard he was kind of anti-sex." Susan assured him this wasn't true at all. "He simply felt that Freud attached too much importance to it." They reached the director's house and the car stopped. Gary thanked her and said goodby. As he started to get out, she said, "When you've finished your interview, I could send the car to pick you up, if you like." Completely astonished, he turned back to look at her. She sat very still, not trembling, outwardly calm, but huddled deep in her corner of the car. "Why should you do a thing like that?" he asked. After a moment, her answer came in a cool voice. "So we can have dinner together."

Gary thought this over and decided that Susan's offer was really much more interesting than the director's. "Okay. I think I've changed my mind, I don't want that houseboy job." He got back into the car and made a move to sit closer to her. She stiffened at once, so he returned to the opposite corner. The chauffeur drove on. After a while she said, "I never stop for people, but for some reason I stopped for you." Gary asked if she had any idea why. "I can't imagine. Except I didn't feel you were dangerous." She withdrew even further. "I'm right about that, aren't I?" He nodded and smiled. She gave a little sigh, and another silence occurred. It lasted until they reached her house. She lit a cigarette and Gary wanted to ask for one, but he didn't. Instead, he passed the time by having fantasies about what she'd be like in bed.

He felt there was something strange about the house, as if Susan didn't really live there; it was all some kind of a trick and the real owner would arrive and turn them out. He knew there were servants, but they never appeared. A radio was playing in the kitchen and the surf beat loudly beyond the sun deck. Susan removed her hat but not her dark glasses, and offered him a drink. Deciding to impress her, he asked for various French aperitifs such as Lillet and Amer Picon, which she didn't have. "Okay," he said, "then I'll have to settle for a Scotch. Just rocks. No water. And please take off those dark glasses."

Rather startled, Susan did so. "She looked a bit older than I'd imagined—maybe *thirty*—but beautiful! Really one of the most beautiful women I'd ever seen." When he told her so, she began to laugh. There was something desperate about her laughter. He felt he had to start making love to her right away, and told her to forget the Scotch. "I took her hands and pulled her close and kissed her, and it was the weirdest sensation. She was very hot for it, but her flesh was completely cold."

They went up to her bedroom. Curtains were already drawn across the windows. The bed was huge, with satin sheets. Again he felt something strange. "I thought, I don't know why, I'm in the bedroom of a woman who takes a really heavy sleeping pill each night. Her body was great. Fantastic! And she was wildly excited. She got between those satin sheets and bared her teeth at me. I hadn't had sex for more than a month and was getting pretty hot myself. But would you believe it? I couldn't get it together. Maybe I'd had too much grass all that time, maybe she was too beautiful—I don't usually go for that, you know— but I couldn't even get it hard. She tried everything, she was really fabulous, then she got very decent about the whole ridiculous thing and insisted on her chauffeur driving me back to Hollywood. When we said goodby, she laughed again. 'It's been coming to this for a long time,' she said. For a long time now it can only be strangers. But strangers I meet through the best people. And now I've finally done this thing I often imagined myself doing. I go to the end, I pick someone up in the street.' All this time she was fingering my buckskin jacket, stroking it, admiring it. 'And it turns out this way,' she said. You can imagine I was beginning to feel pretty awful, and she realized it, and begged me not to. She was very decent that way. She said it wasn't my fault, it was hers, and of course I said that was ridiculous. Then she laughed, and then she didn't laugh any more, and there was that same desperate look on her face. 'It's exactly as I told you,' she said. 'Only in Tibet.'"

Early February arrives another Indian summer. It helps to prolong the routine of that first morning, myself working on the movie script and Gary going off to the beach. Usually he takes his tape machine and cassettes with him, a collection of the Beatles, the Rolling Stones, Dylan, Blood, Sweat and Tears, and Bach played on the Moog Synthesizer. He calls it his "desert island kit." Books are not included. He hasn't finished reading any of the paperbacks in his suitcase and doesn't really intend to, because he suspects that Siddartha and the Dharma Bums and Larry in *The Razor's Edge* all "get somewhere" in the end, and it will frustrate him. Solutions of this kind can never be translated into real life. "Isn't that the trouble with most books? They look so good on paper."

I have decided to let things happen, to talk about them as little as possible. I tell myself this is how Gary wants it, and the whole thing is his idea, anyway: too easy, of course, but for the moment I prefer to avoid difficulties. They'll come whatever I do. Of all the different kinds of signals you can send out, unconscious ones are probably the most effective. The night we met at Loney's, I never even told Gary that I hoped we'd see each other again, yet somehow I encouraged him to make sure we did, because here he is. And here he apparently plans to stay for a while. However, although *he* is never seduced, as he told me, it doesn't take long for the conqueror to start depending on his conquest. Third morning, after breakfast: "I suppose you have to write today?" By making me say yes, he also makes me refuse to spend the day with him. End of the same afternoon: "D'you have plans for this evening?" I've been invited to a party, and he can come too. He immediately looks doubtful. "You're not taking me along because you feel you have to?" No, because I think people will enjoy meeting him, and vice versa. "You mean that?" "Of course." He decides to wear the Cardin suit, but I tell him it's too much. He settles for the Brioni jacket, flowered shirt and tight corduroy pants. At the party he charms a French movie actress, an agent asks if he's ever thought about acting, an artist wants to do his portrait, a starlet gives him her phone number and suggests they go riding together, he disappears somewhere to smoke a joint with the son of the house, and he tells them all his story. They all ask me if there's anything they can do to help. Back at my house in the small hours, he gives a sudden leap in the air like an animal pleased with itself. "I can really hold up with all these people you know, they really find me interesting!" His surprise is genuine; I was wrong to doubt his insecurity. Gary can enter a room and his power of attraction is like gravity, natural and immediate, but while it may seem magical to other people, it confuses him. He wants to be taken "seriously" and doubts that he's worth it.

By dodging the draft two years ago and running off to Mexico, and then to all the other places, Gary may have played out his hand, I fear. He waits now for a new one to be dealt, and (because he met me when he was tired of traveling) hopes I'll deal it. He is too proud to ask, of course, and any kind of maneuvering is not in his line. Technically a criminal, he has no criminal instincts and is really the most innocent of adventurers. "I envy you being a writer, not because I'd like to be one myself—it must be a drag spending all that time alone—but I'd like to have *something* to believe in about myself. And I don't. I never have. I can't find out what to do with my life. A lot of people say, Don't worry, just live it, just *be,* but you can't just *be* when you might get arrested for it."

Like others in this situation, when he's left alone he tends to go to sleep. I come home late from an evening without him and find him naked on the bed, fallen asleep watching TV. He is curled up in the fetal position, and it looks awkward, incongruous and touching because he's so tall.

When the weather changes, so does our situation. A storm wakes both of us up during the night and he asks, "What am I going to do tomorrow?" After breakfast I say I have to start work, and he goes upstairs, listens to his music tapes for a while. About an hour later he returns, stands behind me and puts his hands on my shoulders. "Think I'll go out and drive around." His voice sounds disconsolate. I suggest going to a movie in the evening, but his response is listless. In the middle of the afternoon a small pebble, thrown from behind, hits my typewriter. I look up and see him leaning in the doorway.

"Come here!"

The order is carried out with obvious bravado, and I smile. He grins too, but says, "I've got to talk to you." In the living room he takes his usual chair, glances out of the windows. It has stopped raining but there are low drifting clouds. Everything is gray and blurred; you can't see as far as the ocean.

"There's been something not right between us from the start." He gives me an accusing look. "I can't seem to arouse your genuine interest!" I stare at him, and he says, "You don't *ask* enough!"

"What should I have asked you about?"

"Me. I wanted you to read all those letters, and you did, then you hardly said anything about them. Don't you care how *I* felt about all those other people? Didn't it occur to you that if you didn't know, you couldn't be sure how I felt about *you*?"

"Yes, it occurred to me."

"Then why didn't you ask?"

"I thought I'd find out anyway. Didn't it occur to *you* that if I didn't ask, I was taking you on trust?"

He gazes at me in deep surprise. Finally he says, "No. I never thought about that."

"Did all those other people ask you a lot of questions?"

"Everything, they wanted to know everything!"

"Why was that, do you suppose?"

He looks slightly embarrassed. "You may think this sounds conceited, but they were in love with me."

"Isn't that rather a pity, if you weren't in love with *them*?"

He doesn't answer for a moment. His eyes look very dark and remote. "I've never been in love." The mouth twitches. "If I decided to leave tomorrow, would you be sorry?"

"I can't answer that till it happens."

He jumps to his feet. "Jesus, you don't give a shit!"

"I didn't say that."

He turns away, stares at the floor. "Almost. You wouldn't really try and stop me." His shoulders hunch slightly. "Nobody ever does."

"I'm surprised. A moment ago you said all those people were in love with you."

"Yes, they were. But . . ." He breaks off. "I don't know. Something happens. I'm pretty honest with people and I don't pretend I feel for them what they feel for me. I always tell them it's no big deal, but they believe what they want to believe. Or they imagine I'll come around and see how beautiful and wonderful they really are, and go on my knees to them." He sounds lightly matter-of-fact. "But I never do. Because they're stupid. They're generous in a way, and I have a good time with most of them, but they're stupid."

After a moment, I say: "Well, Gary. I'm afraid I'm not stupid."

His reaction to this is one of his characteristic sudden moves, walking up and down the room and then standing still, as if uncertain what to do or where to go. Then he comes over and sits close beside me on the couch. He gives me a long, almost languorous stare. I notice again that his eyes are deeply empty. "When I showed up out of the blue and asked if I could stay, didn't I throw you? Weren't you pretty excited?"

I have to smile. "I just thought you weren't happy at Loney's and had decided you might be happier here."

Expressionless, he thinks this over. After a glance out of the window, he gets up again. "I may *not* be, if it's still raining tomorrow." He walks out of the room, and a minute later the sound of Dylan singing "I Threw It All Away" comes from upstairs. I feel touched and bored by everything that has just occurred. Why does Gary find it necessary to be declared irresistible? At first I'd thought he was just instinctively, appealingly selfish, like a child or an animal. Now I suspect that for him any relationship is a contest from which he has to emerge the winner. It's his only way of not admitting that people really intimidate him. He conquers his fear by winning the contest, because to lose would mean that he's losing his touch; if that starts to happen, he might find himself alone, abandoned, which terrifies him. Yet he *is,* deeply, alone. If he begins by saying, "This is never going to be *it,*" what choice does he have? I don't understand, or really believe, incapacity to love. It's a textbook phrase, like impotence. But I suppose it's true that you can't love unless you can imagine yourself being loved.

Gary doesn't realize what is happening, of course, because he's very young, and he feels rather than reflects, acts rather than waits . . . But I hate to think this way, it makes me feel old.

Upstairs, the music has stopped. I hear him approach. He stands in the doorway, and something has changed. He wears a smile that doesn't fit. "When you said you weren't stupid, did you mean you never fall in love?"

"Good God, no."

"What happens when you do—did? How do you know?"

Because I don't really want to talk about it, I hear myself becoming rather nervously glib and ironic. "The people I fall in love with are the only ones I never seem to understand. When I'm out of love, I begin to . . . But at the time I fantasize them out of their own reality. Or so they tell me. The kind of obsession Proust wrote about. Or the kind of big deal *you* put down. Wanting what isn't there." Gary continues to smile. "In other words, I blow my cool."

"It's always like that?"

"Too often."

"What a hang-up."

"And what a crock." I'm suddenly appalled by everything I just said. "Any generalization about love is simply the result of being disappointed. When it makes you happy, it's the greatest thing in the world. When it doesn't, find a theory. Anyway, my horoscope says it's all going to change next year. I emerge a stronger character, or less romantic, or something."

"So you're a zodiac freak?"

"A bit. It's like a game that's always on the verge of turning serious."

"What isn't? I'm an Aquarian and my age is supposed to be dawning. So I'm not too sure about astrology yet."

"Aquarians are no good for me, Gary. I'm supposed to stay away from fixed signs."

"If I'm fixed, why am I so restless? Is it just the rain?" He goes to the windows, gazes at the gray world outside, and seems to be speaking to it rather than to me. The wrong smile never leaves his face. "I wonder how long everything can go on. If only I wasn't in this bag, I could take up that agent's offer and be a superstar. Might be fantastic for a bit. Hey, this thing about turning people into fantasies. I never do that! I have to see people *exactly* as they are, otherwise they'd put something over. Like my father. He's a beautiful-looking man, really charming, you want to like him, then he starts talking about ban the criminals and not the guns, cut the hair and drop the bomb. A maniac! Did you ever have the feeling you're like a bomb with the fuse taken out? Or a watch that's stopped? Or . . ." He breaks off, turns back and looks at me. The smile seems vacant now. "You can guess what I did upstairs, can't you?"

The question was telepathic. I was just about to tell him. "A joint. You just did a joint."

"Right. Some kid gave it to me at that party we went to, and I thought I'd put it aside for a rainy day . . ." He glances out of the windows again. "And sure enough it's raining again. Help!" he says loudly. "The sky is pissing! Jesus, let's go to a movie. Any movie. They all look wild when you're stoned." He walks over and pulls me to my feet. "Come *on*!"

As we go out of the front door, he tilts his face to the rain. "And wouldn't it be great if you didn't have to live your life, you could just dream it?"

The day of the open-air concert, Gary woke me up at six-thirty. He said we had to get an early start. Immediately after breakfast, he lit a joint. For the last week he'd been smoking a good deal. "Listen, I can still get a ride if you don't want to come. But I'd rather go with you." The concert was to be given by a new California group who called themselves the Flesh Pots. A year ago they'd been unknown, living like others in a large twenties house somewhere in the Hollywood hills, making music all night, looking for a manager; now their first album was high on the popularity charts. I'd seen them once making a guest appearance on a late-night TV show, but Gary said that was nothing. "They weren't free. They had to tone themselves down." As well as singing, they liked to break things.

Originally the concert was going to be another pop festival, but as so often, half the performers advertised canceled out after most of the tickets were sold. The promoters were left with one hot number, the Flesh Pots, and a couple of less thrilling ones. They decided to make the best of it. The location was a huge rented field, overlooking the ocean, in the middle of some ranchland about eight miles up the coast. As I drove along the highway, we passed the PRIVATE ROAD entrance to Susan's former house. "Shall we look in on the crazy lady?" Gary asked, on his second joint now. "She might really flip if she saw the two of us together." I told him that Susan didn't live there any more. "Too bad." He gave a sudden, meaningless laugh. "Don't worry, I'm not going to crash or anything, it's just a big occasion."

His eyes looked darker, more cavernous than ever. They had the distance of someone listening to messages from a different world. I refused to take a drag, explaining that I wanted to be cold sober for the whole experience, to see it all and not become a part of it. I'd even brought opera glasses. "You're not really with it," Gary said.

"I'm not against it, either," I told him. "I just want to see it."

He laughed and called me basically a voyeur.

About three miles from the site, we turned off on a dirt road and had to stop almost at once. The cars were piling up already, although it was only ten o'clock and the performance wasn't due to start until noon. The traffic jam in itself was extraordinary, almost surrealistic. Most of the cars were painted with psychedelic swirls or decorated with flower decals. Inside them, you saw a kind of collage of flowing hair, stoned-looking eyes, bare torsos, beads, caftans, ponchos. There were various reasons for the pile-up: too many cars, drivers who'd arrived the previous night and were only just waking up, and breakdowns. When a breakdown occurred, the passengers simply abandoned ancient Volkswagens and dilapidated trucks and started to walk. Others honked their horns, then got out and pushed the cars to the side of the road. Two went into a ditch. Nobody cared, except a couple waking up in the ditch. Everyone smiled, and although they were on their way to hear hours of music, the air was noisy with transistor radios.

I managed to park about a mile from the field. A procession streamed across the land, toward the ocean. Inland, the hills were dotted with ranch houses and horses raced about. I noticed how few couples there were, it was tribal, groups of people with their arms around each other. Some wore practically no clothes, although it wasn't warm, patches of heavy cloud in the sky and a pale sun. Many feet were bare. Police cars had been stationed at intervals and cops watched grimly.

In the center of the field was a raised platform. Black, menacing loudspeakers loomed above it. The wind blew in sharp, unexpected gusts and the ocean was a wintry, grayish blue. People sat on the grass, wandered around playing radios, embraced, waited. A redheaded boy who looked about fifteen, with torn denims and long side-burns, came up and asked if we wanted to buy any speed. It was good stuff and he promised the price was okay. A tall young man with hair to his shoulders strolled around by himself, grinning, completely naked. Nobody took much notice.

By eleven-thirty there must have been two hundred thousand people assembled in the field. Gary waved to a few, but said: "I expected to run into more." He was becoming passively stoned, not speaking much, happy to sprawl on the grass and stare. Occasionally, for no reason at all, he laughed. A long way away, on the other side of the field, a scuffle broke out with the police. I don't know what it was about. Standing up, I could see the cops had brought out their clubs and were hustling people away. Again, hardly anyone around us took much notice.

The concert started late, of course, and we had to sit through the inferior groups before the Flesh Pots appeared. The crowd was friendly but unexcited. Many were openly smoking pot now and drinking red wine from half-gallon bottles. Three or four young men wandered around naked. Wisps of light fog began floating in from the ocean. Then people got to their feet, and there was a moment of hush before the Flesh Pots were due to arrive on the platform. It was shattered by an agonizing cry. Not far away I saw a girl writhing on the ground, the child almost due to come out from her body. Friends surrounded her and blocked her from sight, and then a great cheer went up, the sound deafening, amplified on all sides by the loudspeakers that looked like mysterious ruins in the blurred air.

They walked on, five of them, four men and a girl, in various brilliant shades of vinyl, scarlet and orange and white. They wore tight pants and open jackets, and were littered with bracelets, necklets, sequins and beads. Through the opera glasses I could see that the leader was heavily made up; he had black mascara on his eyebrows and lashes and wore lipstick. The girl looked vague and unembellished, her face mainly lost in a tangle of hair.

You could only make out snatches of the words the Flesh Pots sang, the guitars were ear-splintering, but a mood was quickly set: bitter, orgiastic, at times despairing. As the numbers went on, you heard brutal parodies of all kinds of sentimental music, Oriental, soft rock, Dixieland, the Supremes. The mascaraed leader wore a bright, destructive smile. Later, he teased, threw and broke things. A goat was brought on to the platform, bleating furiously. It tried to butt them all, they pushed and kicked it away. I hated this, but the crowd looked beatific, and Gary gave a brief shout of laughter. Then phallus-shaped balloons labeled BLOW ME floated out, followed by grotesque dolls of cops and generals, eyes and teeth and limbs missing. People threw flowers and kissed each other. Gary put his arm around my shoulder. I thought I heard the howl of a newborn baby. One of the naked men walked right past me, penis wildly erect, eyes glazed and meaningless, mouth parted in a smile that showed the gaps in his teeth.

When it was all over, I felt a mixture of relief and letdown. The violence of the ritual subsided to an aimless drifting away. On many faces seemed to be written the question, Where can we go now? Walking back toward the car, Gary and I noticed that an emergency hospital had been set up, with doctors and Red Cross nurses. A few patients were bruised and bleeding, but most of them looked as if they needed bringing down from drugs. Cops watched with a kind of self-satisfaction, and the fog thickened.

Gary slept during most of the drive home. When we got back to the house, he said he was too stoned to get out of the car. I started to help him, but he pushed me away. "No," he said. So I put the car in the garage and left him there. I went to bed early. Sometime in the night I was shaken awake. Gary was laughing. It was dark, I couldn't see his face, but I felt him trembling, almost convulsed, astonished by some secret bliss. Then he sprawled across me and grew gradually calmer. All he said was "I liked it, really."

Next morning was rather like the very first morning, except that it was raining again. After breakfast, Gary said cheerfully, "I'm going out for a while, have a good day, see you later." At the end of the afternoon it was still raining. I'd finished work and was reading and didn't know he'd come back until I heard his voice immediately behind me, calling my name. He sounded different, and when I looked up I saw that he was soaking wet, hair matted, water running off his clothes, a blank, unfocused vagueness in his eyes. He said, "Please help me." I asked what had happened, and he told me he'd taken LSD and was having a very bad trip. He kept on saying that everything felt down and very low, and he wanted *out,* but he seemed more confused and depressed than likely to do himself harm. I took him upstairs, removed his clothes, helped him into bed, reassured him as well as I could, and promised I'd be back in a couple of minutes. The first two pharmacists I asked for glucose gave me rather sly, unpleasant looks and said they didn't stock it. The next offered to place an order, but warned it would take a week. At the health store they were sympathetic, but said there was no demand for it any more. (Did nobody ever want to come out of a trip?) I drove home in the fierce rain and dissolved a pack of granulated sugar in a saucepan of hot milk, then gave it to Gary to drink. He lay in bed, subdued and withdrawn, eyes completely dead. He complained that it tasted nauseating, but drank it all like an obedient child, anxious to please, and after a while began to feel sleepy. He closed his eyes and pulled the sheet over his head.

I stayed in that evening, reading, while he slept. The rain stopped, then a new storm arrived. I went upstairs to see if the thunder had wakened him, but he didn't stir. About midnight, when I was deciding to go to bed, he came downstairs wearing my bathrobe. He looked totally recovered. He smiled, yawned, gave a leisurely stretch. "That was a pretty crazy thing to do, but I felt in a crazy mood. Okay if I put another log on the fire?"

He did so, then switched out my reading lamp. Only the garden lights burned now, putting a glitter on the rain, on weeping, drooping trees. He settled himself on the floor in front of the fire, propping up his head on cushions, and asked for a cigarette. I lit it for him. "When I was fifteen," he said, "I tried all the hard stuff, I shot coke and speed but both of them brought me down. Really *down.* So I felt lucky to have gotten through all that pretty early, and until today I never used anything stronger than hash."

I asked who gave him the LSD.

"Someone on the beach."

"You went on the beach in the rain?"

"No, not today. Someone I met on the beach before. A couple of weeks ago. And I'd met her before that, too. A little hippie kid who had this baby by some guy and lived in that house in the hills I told you about. Now she's living in an apartment in an old building near the pier. I dropped by this morning, and she said she had these capsules, why don't we do it? It's such a lousy day we both need something to make us feel good. I was still kind of high anyway from the concert, but she begged me to do it with her, and there was nothing else around, and when you looked out the window it was like the end of the world." He half closed his eyes. "I don't think I can describe what happened."

"Can you try? I'd like to hear."

"Well . . . D'you have another cigarette?" I gave him one and he said, "Don't light it for me, I want to light it from the fire. I love this fire." He rolled a piece of newspaper into a taper, crouched over the fire and lit the cigarette. I noticed that his hands shook slightly. He didn't lie down again but stayed close to the fire, crouching, holding his unsteady hands toward it. "It was all to do with death. At first it was life, and okay, but then it was all death." From the distance came a snarl of thunder. It startled me, but he seemed hardly to hear it. "She had this single rose in a cracked jar, and it was breathing. But then it died."

When the rose died, so did everything else. The girl was dead, a skeleton on the bed, mouthing words he couldn't hear. The baby in its hammock was quite dead. Gary's blood went cold, his limbs froze and shriveled, and the bones came through. He saw that everything in the little apartment was cracked, beginning with the glass jar, then the walls and ceiling and windows. Gradually the floor split down the middle. He opened a window and leaned out; the sill cracked under his elbows and drowned people floated in the ocean. He himself was dying now, but not completely dead; there seemed a chance of surviving if he could escape. The way was difficult, all the corridors and stairs in the old building began to crumble and give off a sickly moldering smell, but somehow he reached the boardwalk outside and felt the rain. The rain at least was a sign of life, but it was still necessary to hide. It looked safe under the pilings of the pier; they were rotted and slanting but he had the impression they wouldn't actually fall. After he'd taken shelter there for a long time, it seemed that things were mending, although the scars would never heal. He found his car. The blotches on the paintwork were all festering, like a leper's skin, but the engine started. He drove home very slowly, skirting abysses in the road and other cars that hurtled by out of control, their drivers dead.

I asked Gary if I'd looked dead to him.

"No, that's why I thought you could help me. Then I wasn't sure, because after you put me to bed and said you were going out, I felt pretty scared. I knew they put people to bed when they're going to die. But I was so relieved to have gotten back here, and so tired, I thought—well, I've done everything I can, if you don't realize how near death I am, there's nothing more I can do."

"Have you thought a lot about death?"

He shook his head violently. "Not real death. Only the living kind. You know, the whole straight world. *You* must have thought about that, too." Then he wanted me to lie on the floor beside him and look at the fire. He said that a fire at night with the rain outside was one of the most beautiful things in the world, and after what had gone before it seemed an oddly, flatly conventional thing, until he explained that the fire was alive and good to watch after a day of death. We lay side by side for a while, not speaking, and I could feel him subside into a kind of peace. A log broke and spurted flames. He said quietly, without the usual tease and challenge, "I really want to get to know you better. The best way is to read one of your books, and that's what I'm going to do tomorrow. All day tomorrow I'm going to do that, and I hope it doesn't stop raining. Then we'll have dinner and I'll tell you what I know."

I woke late, to the return of sunlight. Outside, the air was so still that I could hear not only each wave as it broke half a mile away on the shore but also the tide sucking it out again. Gary was already up. I felt sure that with the weather clearing he'd happily forgotten his plan of last night and gone down to the beach. In a way, I was pleased. A few hours without him would be good, because we had reached a point at which I couldn't go on letting things happen. A decision had to be made.

Then I noticed the drawers of a chest were open. Looking in the closet, I found his suitcase and clothes no longer there. A few of mine had vanished, too, a couple of shirts, a sweater, a sports jacket. My wallet lay on top of the chest.

He hadn't taken any money, which was somehow right. In Gary's book that would be serious theft, while the clothes were just things that he liked and knew I could spare.

He'd left no message but had made coffee. The pot was still on the stove, half full, lukewarm. The front door stood open. You always had to close it with a slam, and obviously he hadn't wanted to wake me. There were few other traces: unwashed coffee cup in the sink, some sugar spilled on the kitchen counter, a cigarette butt in an ashtray. I cleared them up automatically and was left more with a sense of mystery than of loss. In itself the surprise was so characteristic as to be no surprise at all, but I couldn't understand why he left in secret, why he ran away from me. He'd told me he only did that to avoid a threat or a scene, and he couldn't have expected either from me. I remembered something he'd said last night, just before falling asleep. He asked me why people can become more deeply intimate as the result of a casual attachment rather than a long love or close friendship. I didn't know, but supposed that impermanence had something to do with it. "Right," he said. "When time's running out, you get a touch of fever." Then he turned away from me and curled up in his usual position.

The phone rang. A girl's voice, sounding rather faint and frightened, said: "Oh! Could I speak to Gary please?"

I told her that he wasn't here, and she seemed put out, and asked when I expected him back. I said that I didn't. There was another "Oh!" and then; "You mean he's left? Gone away? For good?"

"It looks like it. He didn't tell me he was leaving, but he's gone."

"I wonder where?"

"I've no idea at all."

"If he's left *you,* I'd have thought he'd be *here.*"

"Where is that?" I asked.

"Oh! . . . Excuse me, I'm a friend of Gary's, my name is Sally."

"Sally O.?" I said.

"That's right. Did he tell you about me?"

"No, just that you'd placed a want ad for him in the *Free Press.*"

"He never answered it," she said, sighing. "He never answers. I just happened to run into him again a few weeks ago. On the beach. I'm living near the pier right now." A baby began howling. She excused herself, then came back on the line. "Was he all right after the trip?"

"Yes. It was bad, but he seemed to get over it."

"Great. I knew it was bad, I could see, but so was mine. I couldn't help. I was wiped out!" She laughed. "I didn't kind of adjust to him not being here any more until this morning. Then I was kind of worried. Listen, I've no right to ask you this, but Gary told me so much about you and I would love to come and see you. Just for a few minutes? I really would appreciate it."

"Okay."

"I'll be right over!"

Sally O. arrived cradling the baby in her arms. I guessed it was about a year old. It looked very thin. "He's sleeping now," she said, "but I'm afraid he may be sick. He threw up earlier." I asked if she planned to consult a doctor. "Oh! . . . Well, maybe I should if he doesn't get better soon."

Gary had described her as a little hippie kid, but she was in her early thirties. She wore a light, semi-transparent caftan, and her body looked lithe and young, very sexual. Yet, in spite of this, and the vague wistfulness, and the long hair trailing down her back, the face was that of an aging flower child. It was delicate but faded. She looked around the room, not seeing it. You felt a disconnection between herself and her surroundings; wherever she happened to be, she was really on her way to somewhere else. "I'm not exactly sure why I came," she said. "D'you have a cigarette?" I gave her one. "All I want is to find Gary," she said, "and you don't know where he is." She gave me a hopeful glance, as if I might possibly have changed my mind.

"No. I told you."

"Why did he go away?"

"I don't know. But he does that kind of thing, doesn't he? He moves on."

She nodded. "Yes, he moves on." I hoped she wasn't going to cry. "But I always told him, if anything went wrong, he should come to me." Then, with a touch of defiance: "I love him a lot. I love him more than anybody. He knows that!" The defiance subsided; she became lost and childlike again. "I thought it was all going to work out yesterday. I mean, if he dropped acid, wouldn't he really *find* me? It happens, you find what you truly want. My cigarette's gone out."

I relit it for her, and she said: "I want to look after him. What can I do?"

"I don't know." It was somehow the inevitable answer to all her questions. "Maybe he'll call you."

"Oh! . . ." For a moment she seemed reassured. "Maybe he will. Listen, I've no right to ask this, but you didn't have a row or anything? You didn't turn him out?"

I shook my head.

"Then . . . ?" She looked bewildered. The baby woke up, blinked at her, gave a sudden enraged cry. "He really must be sick," she said.

A few moments after she left, the phone rang again. "Hello!" he said. "I hope I didn't wake you."

"No. Sally O. was just here."

"That's one reason I called. You didn't tell her anything?"

"I didn't know anything to tell her."

"Right." He laughed. "Anyway, if she tries again, don't even tell her you've heard from me. She's very sweet but I've really had that scene. I had it the first time, but she was so . . . Anyway, it's not healthy."

"I had a wild thought," I said. "It's not your baby?"

There was a long pause. "You must be out of your mind. I'd never do a thing like that. I mean, if it *was* my baby, I'd look after it. Somehow. I'm not irresponsible."

"Of course."

He laughed again. "I believe you're putting me on. Are you very angry with me?"

"No, but I'm sorry you felt you had to clear out without a word."

"You're angry."

"No. It's just that if you wanted to leave, you only had to say. There'd have been no scene, nothing unpleasant."

"I know. That wasn't the reason." He sounded hesitant. "I didn't say anything because I couldn't think of anything to say. Understand?"

"No."

"Well. I woke up early and it was such a beautiful day. And I thought—it was so beautiful too last night, it got to a point where it was just perfect. I mean that! And then I thought, Isn't that the point to move on? You can't top it, you can only come down, like from a crazy trip." He paused again, and I knew he was smiling. "I had a friend who used to say, 'Gary, don't fuck with perfection.'"

"In what sense?"

"Come *on*! You know what I mean."

"I suppose so. Anyway, are you all right?"

"I'm fine. By the way, I took some of your clothes."

"Yes, I noticed."

"You did tell me once I could have that sweater."

"It's all right."

"You probably haven't noticed yet I also took a bottle of Scotch and a bottle of brandy. But neither of them were full."

"That's all right, too. Am I not supposed to ask where you are?"

"I'm . . ." He broke off. "I *could* give you a phone number, except I won't be here very long. But as soon as I'm settled—that sounds unlikely, doesn't it, but you know what I mean?—I'll give you a call. You understand my situation?"

"More or less."

"Listen. *If* I give you a call, and suggest having dinner, what would you say?"

"Yes."

There was another pause. "Good. That's really . . ." He sounded awkward, at a loss, unsure how to bring it off. It was unlike him. "On the move," he said out of nowhere. "Somewhere in the world." Then the old manner returned. "I really am quite glad I met you, and I know you feel the same about me. I may not be the ideal guest, but the great thing about being a guest is, you're bound to win one way or the other. Either they're happy to see you arrive or happy to see you go. Right?"

During the next few weeks, when I met people who'd met Gary with me and they asked how he was and I told what had happened, there was no surprise. It seemed the most natural piece of news in the world. They said things like "Well, he was never quite *here,* was he?" or "Well, I'm sure he'll be all right." Only Sally O. remained puzzled and sad. She called again and asked if I'd heard anything from Gary yet. I told her no, and she gave a long sigh. "Why doesn't he get in touch? Doesn't he *know*?" I asked how the baby was, and she said it was still crying most of the time. She hadn't taken it to a doctor because she'd been too busy.

"I've got to decide what to do. It's time I found out what I'm really about. You know? Stop thinking about Gary, stop looking for him? And go and live up in the mountains?"

I asked how she could go and live in the mountains, and she said she'd met this very beautiful man who invited her up there. "They live like a family up there." She sighed again. "He found this old ranch house that nobody wants.

And it sounds so beautiful . . ." His name was Newt God-son and he wasn't handsome or anything, rather small and too thin, but there was *something* about him. "You *believe* in him, that's what he's got. There are people like that. You know? Just the way they *look,* and the *sound* of their voices . . . He writes songs and he sings them. Beautiful songs . . ." Godson had told her it was no use living in the world any more, it only broke your heart. Up there, in the mountains, they kept to themselves and found each other. They sang and cooked and turned on and tamed wild animals and watched the sun rise and go down.

"You *believe* in him . . ." Her voice ached. "You know he's full of love, the real kind, the kind you have to give to get." Godson had told her that her baby would get better up there, too. He believed in mental power, everything started in the mind. You could almost say he was religious.

I wondered how they all did for money, and she giggled a little. "He says it's okay to steal as long as you only take things you honestly need and don't hurt anybody. He says he'll teach me how. It's like the Indians. They believe in sharing. If a person truly needs something basic, like food, or a few bucks, or a car, or a radio, then he has a *right* . . ." I heard the baby howling. "Don't you agree?" she said. "Isn't it a crime to let people suffer and starve and not get where they've got to go?"

A few more weeks go by, carrying Gary back into my past and into his future. Whichever direction, he is farther away. I go to dinner at Loney's one evening and find most of the people who were there that last evening have vanished too.

The footballer-poet left for San Francisco. Magnette and her boyfriend are on their way to Nepal or Afghanistan, Loney can't remember which. "But somewhere close to the kif and the gurus, that's the point." They had just enough money to get to Istanbul and had heard you could hitch rides on the oil routes from there. The student astrologer has just been busted for selling someone about half a lid of pot, and Loney is very proud of the statement he made in court. "They call it a weed, but Emerson said a weed is only a plant whose virtues haven't been discovered yet." He got three months.

Only the little aviatress remains, alone in a corner, listening to flight signals from the airport on her headphones.

Since spring is always the off-season, Loney says, there are only two new arrivals. I feel that I've met the young man a hundred times before. Slim and tall, palely good-looking, wearing high-heeled boots, he doesn't know yet whether he wants to be a writer, a painter or an actor. "But I'm not going to tie myself down and get in any of those bags before I know they're right for me." The girl is not quite sixteen and has run away from family and school in San Diego, which is Magnette's hometown. She got a lift from a middle-aged truck driver and let him have sex with her as a matter of course. Having heard about Loney from Magnette, whom she knows slightly, she expected to find her at the loft. Now she feels rather stranded. She thinks she would like to go to Nepal or Afghanistan.

During the evening, Loney asks if I've heard from Gary. When I tell him, not a word, he looks rather pleased and produces a postcard that came recently, unsigned, from

Japan. "Think I've just about had this place. Back again soon." It strikes me that if Gary is bothering to make contact with Loney again, things can't be going too well, but I'm relieved that at least he'll always have somewhere in the world to go.

"No, something else came up." This was a few days later, over the phone. "I'm in the hills again. It's not much, just a kind of a guest house. Listen, I want to take you up on having that dinner with me, but my ship's still way out at sea and it'll have to be the other way around. Okay?"

It was a strange, derelict area in the process of being "developed." A steep dead-end road stopped under a cliff. On one side was a sheer drop, on the other land had been leveled and three ugly houses built. Two of them were like glass boxes and the third, almost under the cliff, pseudo-Oriental. There were blinds screening all the windows; it looked closed up. Builders' junk lay around everywhere, garbage cans spilled over with litter. Stuck in the dried mud, encrusted, cartons and bottles were arranged like found objects. Pop music sounded from each glass box. It was dusk. An abandoned car stood by itself near the drop, at least ten years old, the rear wheels missing. Below it, a lighted desert, the city glittered.

To the side of the pseudo-Oriental house an alley led to what looked like a temporary shack, built of wood slats, with only one small window. A motorbike was parked at the entrance. As I approached, a girl came up the alley wearing a leather suit, long blond hair streaming below her crash helmet. She had a delicate, fragile face. She got on the bike and zoomed away, past the litter and the abandoned car, around a sharp corner overhung by eucalyptus trees.

Gary stood at the door to the shack, wearing only a pair of torn, bleached Levis. His hair was shoulder-length again, he'd lost his tan and his face looked thinner, almost gaunt. The eyes seemed more deeply set than ever. He put his arms around me. "Welcome to my pad. Of course, after what you and a few others have accustomed me to, it's not so hot. But I tell myself this is only a phase."

The element of reproach was unmistakable, the implication that people had taken him up and dropped him. I had to remind myself that the opposite was true. The shack was certainly depressing, shaped like a small tunnel, with a mattress on the floor, a makeshift open clothes closet, an electric ring with a battered saucepan standing on it. That was all. Emblematic, hanging against the wall, the Cardin suit and the Brioni jacket and the shirts had survived. I noticed the suitcase half unpacked, on top of some clothes the neat package of letters in its rubber band.

"There's nowhere to sit, so I'll put on some clothes and let's go." He rummaged in the suitcase, found the biscuit-colored sweater. A dark stain disfigured the front. "What the hell," he said as he slipped it on, "take me to some place where the food's really good but they don't mind what you wear. I'll walk in with you and they'll take me for a hustler." He stuck his bare feet into Japanese sandals. I must have been staring at him, because his mouth gave its faint, sudden twitch. "So you think I'm losing my looks?"

"You're thin."

"Not enough bread." He laughed. "It's only a phase," he repeated. "I'm not dead at twenty-two."

I asked about Japan and he said it wasn't the same. He used to enjoy it, especially the subservice of the girls, but now it bored him, even made him feel awkward. "I used to like being so tall there, it made me feel I was Gulliver and they were Lilliputians. This time it was just a drag." When he came back, he met a man who owned a recording company and had a few West Coast pop singers under contract. Having just built himself the pseudo-Oriental house, he'd left on a trip to South America. "You're slipping," I said lightly. "Why didn't he let you live in the house itself?"

An expression came over Gary's face that I'd never seen before. His mouth went thin and hard, almost mean. "That's typical of a lot of them. And if something better comes up, I'll just split. If I do, I hope his house burns down. Screw him, anyway."

At dinner he drank a good deal and didn't eat enough. "Still got your house, then? Of course you have. You've got your house and your work and your life. Everything the way you want it. Lucky you." Then, jokingly, but with an edge of bitterness: "I didn't like to tell you this at the time—after all, it was hardly my place—but you've got everything a bit *too* planned out. You don't want to become rigid. Better watch it."

I asked what signs of rigidity he'd found, and he grinned. But not in the old way. There was something tense, hostile. "You want me to criticize you? You'd like that?"

"No, of course not. Who does? But tell me anyway."

He took a cigarette from my pack on the table, waited for me to light it, then inhaled very slowly. "Just your general attitude. But you can't help it. You're a writer. A word freak. And word freaks are idea freaks. Systems, concepts, you know? Rigid things! They get between you and . . ." He broke off.

"What?"

He grinned again. "There you go. Wanting words, wanting to make it rigid." He patted my hand consolingly. "It's really quite simple," he said. "A blank envelope. But, address it, and it's just another bill, or a love letter. That's why we take drugs. You get there without words."

The *we* struck me as ominous. Was he becoming a spokesman for the drug experience? I asked what he was taking now.

"A little bit of this. A little bit of that."

"Better watch it." Then I remembered something. "But didn't you tell me you tried them all when you were fifteen, and they brought you down?"

"I guess I thought they did. Or did I?" Another grin. "It gets confusing. I'm such a liar."

I wanted to get away. Why was everything he said suddenly so grating and dreary? We drove back to the hills, silent in order not to bore or annoy each other. I reached the dead end, started to say, "Well, Gary," but he put his hand on my arm and insisted that I come into the shack with him. "Please. In spite of my behavior tonight, I don't want you to go yet." His voice cracked. To my astonishment, there were tears in his eyes. I had once thought this unimaginable.

It was chilly inside. He plugged in the electric ring for heating. We sat together on the mattress, leaning against the wall, opposite the only window. It gave out onto the alley and the windowless side of the house. It was like looking through to only another wall. "Know what made me angry?" he asked. "Why I started bitching? The way I caught you staring at me, as if I'd lost my looks."

"I just thought you were—"

"Thin?" He laughed in the old way, wryly cheerful. "Okay, suppose we're not here, we're at your house, and I turn up the way I did the first time. Would you take me in?" Then he put his hand over my mouth. "What a lousy question. Don't answer it."

When he took his hand away, I said: "Answer this if you like. Suppose the draft never existed, you never had that problem. How different would your life have been?"

"I don't know." The reply came automatically. Then he stared at me, no trace of tears in his eyes now. They were cold, without light, two stones set in a face. "Think maybe I could have loved somebody?" He laughed, and mimed the playing of an absurdly romantic violin. "But I *had* the problem," he said, "and my life *can't* be different."

"I wonder. You're not like most people who dodge the draft—"

"I'm not like most people, period," he reminded me sharply.

"All right, I only meant you don't quote Camus. And you don't have any kind of a cause. Isn't it time you found one?"

His face stiffened. "You've got a cause for me?"

"How about yourself? Suppose you make up your mind there's nothing more important?"

"There isn't. How else do you think I've been living?"

"I thought you could do it. But you despise yourself somewhere," I said. "Like a lot of egotists, you're secretly putting yourself down. Why not decide, without any pride or any guilt, that you want to survive? And you don't want to suffer? Then see if—"

"Verbal intercourse!" He shrugged. "Oral communication! Don't you ever get enough of it? You're just talking while I'm . . ."

"What?"

"Somewhere you can't reach. Somewhere you can't talk your way into. Or out of. I've only got two choices. I give myself up and they take over, make me live their way. Or I go on the way I am, which is no good, but the only way they let me. There's nothing else." His tone was final, dismissive. "Anyway, I didn't ask you in for sympathy and advice. I don't mean to be rude, I'm just way past all that crap." He stared at his feet. "I could use fifty bucks, though."

There were forty-five in my wallet and I gave them to him. He acknowledged this with a bare nod that had nothing to do with gratitude or lack of it. A little money had come his way, he could use it. "Had to sell my car," he remarked. "Didn't get much for it, either. It needed a lot of work."

I said that I had to go.

"Yes, you all have to go."

The first time we met, at Loney's place, he'd been determined to play doomed, but it was very different now, because he wasn't enjoying it. The role had become a necessity, like breathing or sleep. I supposed it was why the humor had gone out of his laughter and his smile. He didn't get up but remained on the mattress, head leaning against the wall, staring through the window at nothing. I felt that I'd just paid a visit to someone in jail.

"Gary . . ."

He raised one hand suddenly. It was a wave of goodby that asked me not to say anything more. I could only speak from the wrong side of life. As I walked up the alley, I heard the tape machine playing synthesized Bach. The derelict car confronted me like an apparition, haunting the lights of the city.

Now it has rained again, and been foggy again, and drizzled for a day or two. In the cold and the rain the hitchhikers look like refugees. Some drape themselves in blankets, though their feet are still bare. Finally the desert winds return and the world is startlingly vivid and clear. It won't last long, but that seems part of its intensity. Driving along the rim of the mountains, I pass through wilderness; I started out only half an hour ago, but the empty country feels centuries away. The road twists against sandstone cliffs, occasionally straightens out for the length of a short valley. A barn, an isolated frame house, fences that stop in the middle of nowhere, sheep in the meadows that will be green for no more than a month. For several miles there is nobody about, then I come to a lookout point. People have parked their cars on a soft shoulder and gaze westward, where the peaks of these same mountains emerge from the ocean that covered the rest of them years ago. Now they lie on the bed of the Pacific and are called the Santa Barbara Islands. I gave a ride the other day to a boy in a poncho who believed that much more of California would soon be like these islands, after the earthquake.

After a while I recognize the turn-off that Gary described to me on the phone. A gravel road leads higher up into the mountains. A weathered sign says KEEP OUT, but there's no gate or barrier. The old ranch house appears around a corner. Two barns stand nearby. There are holes in all the roofs. A hundred yards from the house an open gate lies on its side, between two broken fences. Immediately in front of it grows a tract of grass, brilliantly green. Two or three people stand together on it, wearing long robes. From a distance you would take them for members of an exotic tribe.

Without warning, it seems from nowhere, a person appears standing in front of my car. He waves his arms at me to stop. His black hair is worn Indian style, and he wears only a pair of faded sailcloth trousers that reach to his calves. I stop, and he comes up to the window. I notice that he looks very thin and bony, his ribs protrude, and there are mild stains and eruptions on his face and chest. His expression is stony. He asks if I didn't see the KEEP OUT sign and I tell him yes, but I've come to see Gary. He relaxes, goes around the car and gets in beside me. "Oh, it's you. I'll ride with you up to the house." It's very casually done, but he's acting like a guard. I ask his name. Rather startled, he tells me "Chip" but doesn't take it any further. He gazes out of the window, smelling of sweat and something less agreeable, not just dirt.

As we draw up, the figures in long robes are standing, watching, three girls with disheveled hair, faces pale and a little drawn. One has the same faint stains on her skin. A child runs up to her, naked except for a necklace made of desert stones. "Gary's friend," my guard explains. They nod. I feel like a tourist.

A veranda extends in front of the house. Wild flowers have been planted in pots and blankets hung across the windows. My guard says, "You'll find Gary in there," and walks off toward one of the barns. Opening a heavy wooden door, I hear a guitar and someone singing. Inside, however, there's no singer. Four people are sitting on the floor, and a man stands by himself. They don't notice me yet, and I remain in the doorway. The song plays on Gary's tape machine. He and Sally O. are sitting together, their backs to me. The room is rather dark because of the blanketed windows and has no furniture at all. A few mats are scattered on the floor, and tacked to one wall is a travel poster that says INDIA, with a photograph of a golden Buddha. Incense burns somewhere.

Light streaks through a hole in the roof and the man stands beneath it. He listens to himself singing. I know this from the intensity of his expression. Except for being spotlit by the late afternoon, Godson doesn't appear particularly striking. Even his costume, a pair of black shorts and an Afghanistan coat, embroidered goatskin lined with fur, is for these days no more than modestly bizarre. He has a short, wiry body with thin legs, tousled brown hair and a Mexican mustache. His voice is hopeless. The refrain of the song goes, "I'm just the ocean breaking on your shore." Before it ends, he looks across and sees me, bristles for a moment, then seems to remember that I'm expected, and smiles.

The tape finishes to murmurs of approval from the floor. Gary waves. I go over and say hello to him and Sally O., and he hugs me. I notice the baby asleep on Sally O.'s lap. It looks healthier. So, rather to my surprise, does Gary. He's still very thin, but the seediness has gone, in its place an almost wild quality, the look you find in hermits and Gypsies. Godson has it as well, and also a few blotches on his face. I can't see any of these on Gary, which is a relief; but the other girl sitting on the floor has them badly. Gary introduces me to her and her companion, a boy of perhaps nineteen, and they smile very sweetly. Then he takes me over to Godson, who asks at once if I liked the song. His eyes wait with a kind of veiled ferocity. I seem to convince him, because he goes on, "Know anyone I could take it to?" I explain that I'm not in the pop-music world, and he claps me unexpectedly on the shoulder. "One up to you, brother. Don't be *in* any world. Keep out of all those worlds." The girls smile approvingly.

Gary lights a joint while Godson talks on, rambling yet earnest, as if taking me on a quick guided spiritual tour of himself. In a soft, almost insinuating voice he says that the only world in which to live is the world of love. "If you're strong, the others can't hurt you. We're all strong here. Love is the strongest. Yes. *They* think it's weak. No. Strong is gentle, weak is violent. It's the naked ape pulls the trigger. Twenty-seven years in the world, all those worlds— I'm twenty-nine now—and I made no trouble, saying sir to the boss people. I respected the law and I'd have paid my taxes if I'd ever earned enough money to tax. But they still went after me. Know why? They were scared of my strength. Every time I came back to them with love, and they hated it. They hate love. You can't win out there. Too many pigs rushing down the slope." He takes the joint from Gary, swallows, continues talking while he holds the smoke in his stomach. "You understand me." This is made as a statement of fact. "I got your vibrations even across the room. Just don't let them hurt you. Are you strong enough? Can you hold out? Don't forget, all ways lead there. Man and woman, man and man, woman and woman, everything all at once, they all lead there. Love is sacred. You loved Gary. He told me you gave him the kind he never had before. Beautiful."

Surprised, I look at Gary. He nods calmly, and I suppose that a legend has been created. Mysteriously blessed, Gary has inspired a great love. Well, of course he would like that. I feel glad that I didn't let him down after all, but unprepared for this new role.

Godson seems to intercept my thoughts. "Sometimes you don't know how much you love. But the other knows, and it stays forever. Yes. That's why real love can't die. They try every way to kill it, but they can't stop it no more than the sun coming up. No." Then, with a sigh: "Maybe you're thinking it's not difficult to love Gary, because he's a beautiful man, you naturally want someone beautiful. That's nothing. They all love Gary because of that." A glitter of pride appears in Gary's twilight eyes. The legend grows. "But you loved him in spite of he was beautiful. That takes . . ." Godson seems suddenly to lose track. "I'll play you more of my songs if you like. Any time." He raises his hand in a gesture of vague benediction, and wanders off.

The girls stare rather wistfully as Gary leads me outside. The others in their long robes are still there, like statues on the grass. They gaze at Gary in the same way. He smiles to himself, takes my arm. We walk on, toward the fallen gate and broken fences. The wind has dropped, the sun is leaving, and the dusk will be slow. There is suddenly nothing except the glassy, fainting light, the mountains crouched silently above us, and a huge sky. Lower down, the lights of houses are coming on, but too far away to matter, to pierce the darkness when it falls here. The stillness contains an almost terminal solitude.

It used to be much simpler. Either you withdrew passively to simple hills and lived in peace the way nature is supposed to, or you chose militancy, staying in the world to protest against it, making noise and trouble. Now, withdrawal itself seemed to be turning militant. According to Godson, anyone who stayed in the world was weak, passive, a dupe. The true strength and the only action were up here in the mountains, protected by guards. Maybe Godson was all for love, but he behaved like a priest demanding followers. Could you leave without betraying him? I suspected that Godson really knew much less about love than Loney, who didn't want his band of people to follow him, but left them free to go wherever they wanted.

"Well, he raps a bit but I don't pay too much attention," Gary said. "And you've got to understand this great thing he's done. You live in a situation where the pressure's off. You feel safe because you know you're doing the only possible thing." He leaned on the fence, gazing at the mountains. It was so quiet, I could hear myself breathe. "When Sally tracked me down and dropped by that place where I was living, or dying, she told me she was coming up here and I thought, Jesus, it sounds crazy. Then I thought, but it's crazy where I am right now. And when I got here and listened to Godson, this beautiful feeling started. Free! He explained how *there's no future*. The future is fear and who needs it? Only the anxious pigs out there." He pointed down to the lights, to another place that wasn't for living. The dusk was making him into an outline, he grew diffuse and apart, like a shadow. I didn't want to argue, to wonder whether he was really free or just possessed by something new. I didn't want a feeling of sadness or loss. All these things seemed irrelevant. Somebody has said that unless he was a genius, a rich man could never imagine poverty. I supposed that without genius a hopeful one could never really imagine despair.

I said, "Well, okay, but why doesn't Godson do something about the clap?"

"You only get it if you join in." Gary sounded surprised. Then he grinned. "Everything all at once, to get there, maybe it's great for them, but . . . Sally and I don't go that way." For a moment he sounded prim and reformed, like someone talking about the neighbors. "So it's not our problem." He gave a sudden contented stretch. "But could you see how they all *want* to make it with me? Even Godson, and I thought at first he was completely straight . . ." The idea of being desired by Godson struck me as nothing to celebrate, but it reassured Gary. Maybe none of the people here would ever send him love letters, and there'd certainly be no invitations to Mexico or Europe, but he was back in a place where they begged him, and he didn't have to worry about losing his touch.

"What about the police ever catching up with you? Do you think about that any more?"

He shook his head. "No reason. That's the future, and it doesn't exist."

Night fell and the stars came out, icily bright. Gary took my arm again. "Come over here, I want to show you something."

A little farther up, near the fence, stood an old telescope on a tripod. "Godson only asks one thing when you come up here to live. Steal something for him. Like a kind of an offering. I wasn't going to come back with any ordinary piece of junk like a radio or a guitar or a billfold. So I started prowling around houses at night to see what I could find. This telescope was in some astronomy freak's backyard and it spoke to me. Think it's too weird?" He smiled at me with the innocent adventurer's expression. Asking me up here, I knew already, was a kind of ceremony, showing me his newly discovered self. Now we seemed to be approaching the heart of it.

He put his eye to the lens and tilted the instrument up at the sky. "Fantastic! The only other worlds I want to go to. Now see what you can see."

He stood aside for me with a low, ironic bow. The moment turned into something else, a solitary remembered fragment of a dream. It was as if I'd just wakened up haunted by it, wondering how I'd arrived at this clear, vaguely scented darkness, why Gary wanted me to look through his telescope, and knowing it was somehow a gesture of farewell. I saw the stars come nearer. They shivered and that was all. I pointed the telescope down, then moved it slowly from right to left, starting with the farthest distance after the sky, an area of night that had to be the ocean. I followed the land as it swept upward and saw dense patches of nowhere stabbed by lights, sometimes a concentration, sometimes single. Closer to where we stood lay the next range of hills, not as high, and a deep canyon away. Near the top of them began a darkness that seemed as if it would go on forever. I stopped the telescope at the edge of it. One light burned there like a signal, and I think it came from Susan Ross.

LORA CHASE

A solitary figure walked away along an empty road, under a bare white sky, toward a blank horizon. She wore black. Below, in huge sloping elongated letters: ON THE ROAD TO GOD KNOWS WHERE. I think it was winter and remember the real sky as that overhanging London gray, hardly daylight at all. I was ten or eleven years old then and passed the billboard every day on my way to school. The film was about one of those women of mystery who finally disappear forever on a dangerous foreign waterfront, or die in the arms of an illegitimate son they "spare" by never revealing who they are. I went to see it by myself on a cold Saturday afternoon and was spellbound by the actress, who was beautiful in a rather fine, aristocratic way and far more mysterious than the woman she played. Her voice had a smooth low quality somehow perfectly pitched for lying. She was passionate without being explicitly sexual. You felt sure that she used the rarest, most elusive perfume. And no matter how candidly, longingly she rested her eyes on an actor in a scene, or on myself in one of those direct staring close-ups with music, she gave the impression of really watching something or someone else beyond, farther away, out of reach. For a long time afterward I imagined that she was my mother, fascinating, devious, troubled, with a secret life that she never confided to my father (if he *was* my father), only to me. It became very important to see all her films as they came out. She introduced me to a world in which people always betrayed people, tables were turned and appearances reversed. Intrigue and elegance at the end turned horribly sordid. Games became cruel. One film revealed her as a murderess of exquisite manners and duplicity, and I thought she could go no further. Then, in another, the gentle chatelaine of some Gothic mansion overlooking the sea turned out to be a vindictive ghost. She haunted me for months.

Later on, in "real" life, she became an alcoholic, then a Catholic. There were no more films. She had gone. After a long separation I happened on her photograph in *Paris-Match*. She must have been at least fifty, but looked more beautiful and secret than ever. She was living with a minor dictator in Central America. Both the affair and the dictator lasted only a few months. The years that followed must have been spent on the road to God knows where. When I first came to California I heard that she'd been living in Mexico City, then that she'd bought a place in Hawaii. I wrote to an actor friend who was on location in the islands. He made inquiries and could find no trace. At the Screen Actors' Guild they said her membership had lapsed since 1955.

It was strangely difficult to meet anyone who'd known her, and disappointing when I did so. One evening I was at dinner at the house of an actress who'd appeared in a film with her, a rather pretentious *grande dame* from the theater who spoke with a British accent and came out to Hollywood while they still made movies with repressed unmarried aunts, nuns and sinister housekeepers. On the dining-room wall, spotlit, hung a painting of herself as Sarah Bernhardt. "Oh, *Lora* . . . ?" A faint frown implied that I was asking for a remote, unimportant memory. "I never knew her well, of course." The *of course* was eloquent. "Not at all a classical actress, no, a complete product of the motion picture, a face, a really rather beautiful girl—well, not exactly a girl, she must have been forty . . . But rather beautiful. And sad, I believe, what happened . . ."

Like others, she would not be drawn. At another dinner party, one of those movie directors in their late sixties, accomplished veterans who have done everything from early gangster films to musicals to World War II love stories and are more interested now in playing the horses: "Lora Chase? Yeah, I did a picture with her, let's see, around '40, maybe '41. *Secret Wife?* No . . . *Dangerous Interlude.*" I tell him it was called *The Parting Shot* and he takes my remembering it as a personal compliment, which it's not. "Right! I've made a lot of pictures, see, some of them get away." Cigar smoke in my face. "Very good actress, Lora, easy to work with, knew her lines, took direction. Very easy. But kept herself to herself. You never got close. Maybe that's why she never became a real star. People like to get *close*. Is she dead? Nice talking to you."

Occasionally one of her old films is shown on TV, but always at the insomniac hour, three or four o'clock in the morning. Once I make a point of staying up for *The Parting Shot,* but the program has been changed and there's an early Tarzan picture instead. At a bookstore specializing in literature about the movies and all kinds of Hollywood memorabilia, I find an old studio photograph, but it's too conventionally glossy and posed, without resonance, and I don't buy it. One of her leading men, with whom she made two films in the Forties, now lives in retirement on a date ranch outside Palm Springs. However, a writer working on a book about Hollywood, a fanatic who knows everything, tells me that he is ill-humored and a transvestite who wanders angrily around the desert in long evening gown and picture hat with feathers. "Are you sure? He always had a mustache." "They often do." I don't feel ready for this. It has begun to seem appropriate, anyway, that Lora Chase remains a shadow and a question.

So as years pass she occurs to me only in passing, and now I'm at another house on the beach, on a hazy Sunday afternoon with the colors bleached out like a memory, sky and ocean in a hesitation of palest blue and gray: a simple, small, untidy living room, a divan with a Mexican blanket, rattan furniture, a mandala poster on the wall, and a handful of people in their twenties, most of them sprawled together on the divan. I am thinking of leaving soon, impatient with long silences and the inevitable trail of grass.

The house belongs to a painter I know who used to live up in Topanga Canyon, then moved to the beach during a mildly freaked-out phase of doing everything except paint. Frail and peaceful in his hophead period, he is assembling a collection of exotic mail-order objects that lie around the room, oddly lifelike plastic disembodied vaginas known as Instant Pussy, "meditation" candles that drip wax in scented rainbow colors, bumper stickers that say ANOTHER

FAMILY FOR PEACE and BE HAPPY, a huge penis of hard flesh-colored candy called the Cocksickle. On Sundays people drop by the house and smoke, leaf through health-food magazines and paperbacks about Edgar Cayce, stare out past the balcony to the afternoon. It is very innocent and affectionate here, full of generalized love. The long silences tell you, *everyone is fine, everything is beautiful, the rain is beautiful, and so is the sun and the Cocksickle.*

However, more talk suddenly develops because of a girl wearing a black leather suit. When I arrive, she is sitting by herself on the balcony, her back to the room, crash helmet on the floor beside her. Later on she comes inside and I recognize her as the girl who walked out of the alley and rode away on a motorcycle the evening I visited Gary at his shack. She recognizes me too, smiles and sits by herself on a stool. The motorcycle outfit doesn't make her look at all butch; she's like someone trying on her older brother's costume. Long sun-streaked hair flops across her face and she constantly brushes it away. Her eyes are timid, a gentle gray. No one introduces us, they don't bother with things like that. She leans across to the painter, says something quietly in his ear, and they begin a low whispered conversation. After a while she raises her voice unexpectedly and asks: "So anyway, who needs reality?"

People look up, but nobody answers. A long pause follows. Finally the painter says with a sigh, "But what is reality?" She smiles and shakes the hair out of her eyes again. "I don't know," she tells him. "Maybe reality's not the word I mean. I mean real things, facts, situations." She refers to them with a slightly indignant surprise. "All the people who think they know what ought to be done. And all the things and people they want to do it to. I've been through too much of that and it just gets in the way."

Another long pause. On the beach, a dog is barking. The painter yawns, then asks reluctantly, "In the way of what, honey?"

She hesitates. "The other place." She blinks, gives him a hopeful look. "Know what I mean?" When he shakes his head, she goes on, "It's better there. Nothing's good or bad. You don't have to tell them you didn't ask to be born in it. You're there because you choose. You made it up."

The only reaction is a few heads shifting away from her, eyes searching for something to look at, the geometric pattern of the mandala, the arrows woven into the blanket, BE HAPPY. She has gone too far, she wants to confide and explore this creation of her mind, and nobody cares. The afternoon is supposed to continue in the silence that repeats, *everyone is fine, everything is beautiful.* I look at her and am suddenly interested, not particularly for what she's said, or for her connection with Gary, whatever it was, but for the eagerness in her eyes, so vulnerable, so incongruous with her outfit. She senses this and looks back at me as if I'm her last chance.

"Do you have a name," I ask, "for the other place?"

"That's its name."

Somebody laughs vaguely on the divan. "She trips, she just wants to trip all the time."

"You're wrong!" Her voice is fierce for a moment. "I'm not talking about some kind of *escape.* The other place is just as . . . as—" she stumbles—"as real as where we are now."

He laughs again. "But who needs reality?"

She shrugs, gives up, and wanders out to the balcony again. He says, "Has she gone to the other place?" but the joke falls flat.

I ask the painter who she is, and he sighs again. "I don't know." He repeats the question to the others on the divan. Heads are shaken, eyes go vacant, then a girl wrapped in a serape says, "Oh, you've seen her before. She came with Jim. She went with Jim." She picks up the candy penis, licks it and giggles. "Hey, pretty delicious, why don't they all taste like that?" An aimless dialogue begins with the man who laughed. He asks, "Hasn't Jim gone to Santa Fe?"

"Yes, I think he's in Santa Fe."

"Then she's not going with him any more."

"I guess not."

"Then she came by herself today."

"On her bike?"

"I guess so."

"Why?"

"Hell, I don't know."

"Maybe you ought to apologize."

"Why?"

"You laughed at her."

"No, I just laughed *at*."

"*At?*"

"You know, not at *her*."

"Maybe she doesn't think so. You ought to explain."

"Let it alone."

"People can be very sensitive."

During this, I glance out at the balcony. She leans over the railings, smiling, waving, trying to attract the attention of the dog that still barks.

•

The sun was low and faint behind the haze, and the beach looked very pale. It felt chilly. She looked up as I came out. "You knew Gary, where did he go?"

I told her about Godson's place in the mountains. She nodded. "People always go off to places. Jim—that's the last guy I went with—he left for this place near Santa Fe. A commune thing. They worship the rising sun, I guess. You think Gary will be okay up there?"

"He seemed happy."

"They always say that when people go off." She looked suddenly anxious, as if she didn't want to be misunderstood. "But maybe it's true. I only knew Gary a couple of weeks. It wasn't important. He's got no imagination."

"Why do you say that?"

"I never saw any sign of it, that's all. He seemed to *want* to hang around in that rotten situation. I think that's kind of dumb. I used to tell him to . . ." She broke off and gestured toward the room. "Did I make any sense in there? It's always hard to explain. I just have this thing about *going into your own mind.* You know. Just going *in.* Following it wherever it takes you." She laughed. "Some people say that's going *out* of your mind. But the people who say that, they're—well, *here.* And not liking it much. So who's putting down who?"

Then, almost formally, she introduced herself. "My name is Keelie Drake. Hello. Nice to meet you." We shook hands. She asked what I did, and I said I was a writer. She asked what I'd written, looked vague when I told her, but pretended to remember one of the titles. "I think I read it. You live at the beach?"

"Overlooking it."

"I live in the hills. You know what *they* overlook. Except, my place doesn't have any view at all, you wouldn't know there was a city down there. Just a high wall covered with ivy. Not even when the tree . . ." She broke off again, rather quickly. Her thoughts seemed like a wind that was constantly changing, she never knew from which direction to expect them. "But I guess they liked it private in those days."

"Who?"

"I'm sorry. It's always hard to explain. This place where I live—the first boy I ever went with here found it—it's a kind of a guest house. I think they call it a *lodge*. Anyway, it goes with the bigger house. In the grounds. The bigger house is empty. No one's rented it in ages. It belonged to some movie star years ago, you probably never heard of her, I'm not sure I ever had until . . ." She broke off again. "But it's so difficult to know what you remember, to be sure about it. I mean, you think you've forgotten, you never heard it, and then . . . Her name was Lora Chase," she said. "I guess she went away, too."

I stared at her.

"I wonder why she didn't sell it. But maybe she tried and nobody wanted to buy it. You're looking at me in a kind of strange way," Keelie said. "Is something wrong?"

"No." I told her about my long-ago connection with Lora Chase that was not even a connection, just a billboard and a few movies that impressed me as a schoolboy, and some fantasies, and how when I came to California nobody knew where she was, or could even tell me anything about her. Keelie listened with a concentration that made her face rigid, like stone. Then she said, "Jesus!" and went paler than white and swayed, and I thought she was going to faint. "No, it's okay. It's just . . . What kind of a person can she be? Why does she pick on people? And how can anyone do a thing like that when they're *not* . . . ?"

I smiled. "I never felt she picked on me. There was just a way she looked on the screen—"

"But she brought you here," Keelie said with absolute conviction. "To Hollywood, U.S.A. I mean you're here, aren't you? Thousands of miles away from where you were born, at the other end of the world."

"That's wild, she had nothing to do with it. I came here because—"

"Oh, I'm sure you had a reason. But I'm not talking about *facts*. Although it happens to be a fact you had this thing about her, and now you're here. And you said she *taught* you things."

"Only in a manner of—"

"About people tricking each other. And appearances turning into . . ." Her voice sounded obstinate now, almost sullen. "Why should you learn things like that from *her*? Why not from real people or books?"

"Sometimes—"

"Why only from her movies? You said they were just wonderful trashy movies."

"All right, let's leave it there for the moment," I said. She was biting her thumbnail, and a look of childish pleasure crossed her face, as if she'd gained her point. "But how could she pick on *you* when you'd never even heard of her? Or knew what she looked like?"

"Well . . ." Keelie frowned. "I came here from Long Beach, you see. That's only thirty miles away, but now it feels like . . ." The anxiousness returned to her eyes; I must have looked as if she were losing me again. "I'm going to try and explain." She made it sound unlikely that she'd succeed. "There's nothing really wrong with Long Beach. I guess it's not the worst place. But I thought I'd go crazy if I didn't get away. My parents had no imagination. And their friends were just the same. And whenever I met anyone I liked, they'd always be leaving for L.A. Or somewhere."

Her father was a tax consultant, she told me, and her mother liked to gamble, driving twice a week all the way to Gardena, to an illegal private casino in a councilman's house, and losing more than they could afford. Still, they managed to send her through school somehow, although she wouldn't have minded one way or the other, she could never get interested in school. When they told her she had to train for a job, she couldn't get interested in that, either. One day she left a note on the kitchen counter: *I'm going to try it in L.A.* She walked out with a few clothes and belongings stuffed inside a laundry bag that she carried like a pack on her shoulder. She had only twenty dollars, but it didn't bother her. She stood at the freeway entrance with the laundry bag over her shoulder, and got a ride from someone driving to San Francisco. He dropped her off at the corner of Santa Monica Canyon and the coast highway, opposite the beach.

A cloudy day, the wind blowing in quick, sudden gusts. She went into a liquor store and bought some potato chips, found her way through the tunnel under the highway to the beach, sat down on the cold sand. There were few people about. Some boys played volleyball. Bits of rubbish, newspapers and empty cartons drifted past in the wind.

She munched her chips. In the old days, you ran away to Hollywood because you wanted to be in the movies, now you just wanted to be free. She felt free already. Her mind became pleasantly light and empty, like one of the cartons blown along just above the level of the sand. She gazed at the ocean for a while. Finally, drowsiness arrived and she closed her eyes to a mew of gulls.

"That was the first time," she said.

"What?"

"You know how it is when you close your eyes and you're relaxed and not thinking about anything special? You always *see* something at first, maybe just dots and patterns, or a flower, or a place you remember. I saw this woman's face. More than her face, head and shoulders like a shot in the movies. In color, too."

Keelie had never seen the woman before. She was about thirty-five—"beautiful like someone in a painting, or in the movies, know what I mean, really wonderful-looking but not to touch, not *close*?"—and wore a fur-trimmed jacket that seemed much too elegant for State Beach. She looked at Keelie in a friendly but amused way, as if wondering, Now what can *you* be doing here? Startled, Keelie opened her eyes. Naturally the woman who had never been there had vanished. However, in the space where she ought to have been, a young man stood looking down at Keelie. He was about twenty years old, with dark untidy hair, wearing a turtleneck sweater, chinos, a pair of rimless glasses with the lenses lightly smoked.

They began talking. His name was Luke. She described her curious experience when she closed her eyes, but he didn't seem particularly interested. He wanted to tell her about being a student and taking part in a demonstration against the war in Vietnam. It was peaceful until the police were summoned to the campus and ordered everyone to disperse. They refused, and suddenly there was a brawl, and rocks were thrown, and some idiot lit the fuse of a hopeless amateurish bomb that failed to explode, and the police put on gas masks and used Mace. Luke told her about the experience of Mace. He'd been blind the rest of the day, his eyes ached and wept for three days afterward. When he asked Keelie what she was doing on the beach, she explained that she'd come to L.A. to be free. He laughed and said that was impossible in America. She didn't agree with this. You could be free anywhere. When Luke asked what she meant by freedom, she realized that she'd never properly thought about it. She tried now to decide what freedom was, and came to the conclusion it had something to do with that moment before she closed her eyes. She had felt then, sitting by herself on the beach, that anything was possible. Happiness seemed the natural state. She'd had the same feeling listening to music, especially in conjunction with a psychedelic light show. There was a place in Long Beach where beautiful, fantastic images shifted and dissolved on a screen to the sound of vibraphones and auto harps and Oriental instruments. Luke gave another laugh and dismissed this as much too private. To be just an artist these days, to hide in your imagination, was so weak. Why didn't she care about the real world? He tried without success to excite her about politics and the need for revolution. "Oh, I'm sure you're right and there has to be a revolution," she said, "but it's just not the kind of thing I want to get involved with." Violence disgusted her. Besides, you couldn't deny the other place. It contained so much that was beautiful and important. She smiled and touched her forehead with her finger. They continued to argue. Luke grew furious with her for believing in astrology. "But it didn't matter. We dug each other, really." It started to rain and he drove her back to his place, up in the old section of the Hollywood hills.

A great elm overshadowed the entrance to a driveway. The wrought-iron gates were tall and heavy, you could hardly see through them. Ivy covered a thick wall. The solitude appealed to Keelie at once, then she wondered how a revolutionary student could afford to live there. It looked like an estate. However, he rented only the lodge just inside the driveway. It had two small rooms, a kitchen and shower. The main house had been empty for a long time, and Luke told her it belonged to a movie star whose name he couldn't remember and who left town years ago. She learned the name from one of Luke's friends, but it meant nothing to her.

She lived with Luke for three months and tried for his sake to get interested in revolution. "But it really made me—well, it tied me up inside. I thought, It's great they go out there and fight for all those things, but it wasn't where I belonged. But sexually Luke and I were beautiful. That's where we really met, in the other place, in the middle of the night." It ended on the steps of a lecture hall at the university. Luke had persuaded Keelie to come with him and a group of students to block the entrance and make it impossible for the Governor of California to go inside and deliver a speech. They refused to leave. The Governor called them hooligans over the P.A. system, and the police arrived, and angry fighting broke out, and Keelie was dragged away by a cop. A veil lifted. She screamed more with terror than pain, because it seemed that nothing separated her now from blood and panic. She came to lying on the grass, a wet cloth over her face. When she asked for Luke, no one could find him. There was no reason to suppose, when she got back to the lodge, that she would never see him again.

She climbed into bed and tried not to think about anything, to escape forever from what had happened. After a while her mind cleared, she was no longer anywhere, blank and drifting. When she felt herself floating into sleep at last, the woman's face appeared. This time she stood right outside the main house. The front door was open. She looked at Keelie with what seemed to be enormous sympathy, though from a distance. She seemed to be saying, You poor little thing. When Keelie opened her eyes, no one was there, of course, but she knew for certain now that the woman was Lora Chase, because she'd turned away and gone back into the house.

Keelie got out of bed and walked up the driveway. The front door was closed as usual. She broke a window at the side and climbed into the kitchen. Somehow, she felt immediately disappointed. No particular atmosphere or invitation existed there, only the usual desolate vacuum of houses that have been empty for a long time. It was like outer space without the view. Not that she'd expected to *see* anything; but there was a lack of vibrations, of any kind of life, the place seemed completely indifferent and extinct. In one of the bathrooms she found an old cosmetic jar with some dried make-up inside, like ancient mud.

Days passed, Luke didn't come back and no one knew what had happened to him. Maybe he went to San

Francisco, he'd talked of going to San Francisco. Keelie had nowhere else to live, and she liked the lodge and the rent was cheap. She got a job at a store off Hollywood Boulevard called The Rummage Sale, specializing in rather freakish clothing and objects, old fur coats, Victorian boots, wigs, printed silk lamp shades, accordions. Ordinarily, serving in a store would have struck her as drab and unfree, but the atmosphere was casual and the customers mostly refugees from the planned, functional world, with endless time to browse among rabbit-fur bags and phonographs with horns. Around the corner was the bookstore with movie posters in the window. During one lunch hour she went in to ask if they had any pictures of Lora Chase. There was only one—it made her look unexpectedly ordinary—but she recognized her visitor. She tried to find out more from the real-estate agent to whom she paid her rent, but he could only tell her that his client had gone away several years ago, leaving the property in his hands. Occasionally he showed people around, but no one wanted to rent or buy. A rock group almost took it once. A gardener appeared twice a week. When a crack appeared in the cement, the agent had the swimming pool drained. He wrote to Lora, care of a bank in New York, asking what to do. She never replied. That was three years ago. The pool remained empty, with its great crack across the middle and the trees dripping leaves into it.

"So you kept on thinking about her? You expected to see her again?"

"Not really. Although I knew I would."

There seemed to be an aimless, suspended promise in the air. It gave her the feeling that anything was possible, although nothing happened. She liked the carnival atmosphere of the Boulevard. It was too exotic to be sad, just an extension of the store in which she worked, with its tarnished window displays and perpetual sales, unemployed movie extras dressed as if to answer a call issued thirty years ago, old ladies with elaborate tote bags and parasols, angry-looking boys encased in leather, fat men who sweated for hours in doorways, and the sideshows, the man who lay in a coffin, a stake driven through his black cloak to his heart, advertising the opening of a new Horror Museum, the religious group with robes and shaved heads, beating tambourines and handing out brochures. All these trudged and loitered along sidewalks imprinted in gold with the names of stars, they stepped on ghosts and shadows.

Outside a store called, simply, Cut Rate Drugs, some fragments of broken glass glittered on the pavement. Stepping carefully around them, she noticed the name "Lora Chase."

Jim picked her up in a coffee shop. They had both gone by themselves to see the movie playing next door. He had reddish hair, a drooping mustache, a faded pink linen suit, a motorcycle, and wanted to join a commune in New Mexico. After they went to bed together at the lodge, he talked of feeling a oneness with the universe, clear skies and the purity of water from a spring. Later, Keelie was just falling into sleep, weightless and happy, when Lora's face appeared again. She was in the room this time and shook her head slowly in what seemed to be amused disapproval. Keelie wasn't sure whether this was a reaction to Jim, or to the idea that you found oneness in spring water. For the first time she really wished the face would stay for a moment and explain. Then she dismissed this as absurd, and even felt a twinge of resentment. Was this unknown woman in some way trying to *interfere*? It had never occurred to her before that she might not be a friend.

Luke's clothes still hung in the closet; she hadn't liked to clear them out. Next morning, because the night had been so sexually beautiful, she gave them all away to the Salvation Army, except for a suede vest that Jim said he liked.

"Did you think about Lora then?"

"I hope this doesn't sound crazy, but I wanted her to know how I felt."

Jim had a little money from somewhere, from his parents, she supposed. (Keelie had never got in touch with hers.) He had a part-time job, too, cleaning swimming pools, but he was putting this money away. It was taken for granted that when he was ready to leave, Keelie would go with him. At the last moment, without really knowing why, "No," she said, "I think I'll stay on here." There was no scene, because they were always completely free with each other. They just made fantastic love for the last time. "Maybe it's always the greatest when you know it's the last time." He left her his motorcycle so she could ride away if she changed her mind.

After he'd gone, Keelie sat on the bed. It was early morning and very still outside. She closed her eyes. At the time she didn't realize it, but unconsciously she must have been waiting for Lora to appear again and give her a sign. When nothing happened she felt abandoned, almost tricked. During the day, at work, she had a sense of confusion and loss. It ought to have been because of Jim, but on the way home she stopped outside the drugstore and stared at the name in letters of gold.

Soon she became used to being alone again, as she had been after Luke disappeared. A girlfriend said to her, "Aren't you sad because both Luke and Jim went away?" and she thought it a very foolish question. Nothing, however beautiful, was permanent. When you accepted this, you started to become a truly free person. She was young and wanted as many experiences as possible. She found that she could go inside her own mind, and it was like entering a cave of love.

Riding home from work one evening, she reached the lodge and cut off the motorcycle engine. A moment later, somewhere in the street below, a shot rang out. She hurried out of the driveway and saw a man staggering up the street toward her, blood pouring from the sleeve of his jacket. Frightened to offer help and ashamed of her fear, she simply stared at him. He walked on as if he hadn't even seen her. A few nights later she was just going to bed when she heard another shoot-out. In the silence that followed, she waited for some acknowledgement from the world, shouts, footfalls, a police siren, anything. As before, nothing happened. There was no report in the newspapers of either incident, and she supposed that so many occurred, they only wrote up the best. Another time, a girlfriend was driving her home from a party at about one o'clock in the morning. They passed a car standing in an empty street. It was high up in the hills and no houses nearby. The headlights were on, though burning a little dimly, and the driver slumped over the wheel. Keelie made her friend stop. When she touched the man, she knew that he'd been dead for some time, perhaps two or three days. They discussed whether or not to report it, and her girlfriend said, Better not. It was another incident that the newspapers never mentioned.

Going to bed, she wished not to be alone. She knew of course that violence and death happened everywhere, all the time. When you read about them in the newspapers, as you might read about the weather, they somehow became all right. "But when you happen on shoot-outs and dead people, when they seem to be there in front of your eyes, and then it's like they never existed, it gets scary. You wonder how much more goes on that nobody knows about. You even wonder if you really saw the whole thing, or just imagined it. My girlfriend didn't help by saying, 'Well, Keelie, *I* never touched that man, I just took your word for it.'" Late the following night, she rode up to the deserted street in the hills. The car had gone. There was still no mention of it in the morning papers. So either it never happened, or they knew but weren't telling. For the next two nights she slept very badly, then a friend gave her a joint. She smoked it and took a couple of Miltowns that her employer had offered. The combination worked. She began to float in the luxury of approaching sleep.

The moment she closed her eyes, Lora's face was there. She stood in the street below the house. It must have been a cold night; she wore a fur coat and held the collar tightly around her throat. You could see her breath in the air. Her expression was almost beatifically calm and reassuring, her lips parted in a slight, cryptic smile. "I guess there was no connection, but I started smiling too. She made me think,

If we got to read *all* the gruesome things that were going on every day, could we stand it? Wouldn't we go crazy?"

When she woke next morning, her mind felt so elated and clear that the sky outside her window stunned her with its purity. It was like the first day of Creation. That glimpse of Lora, her smile as fugitive as a bird flying, her drift of breath like a magic exhalation in the night, now seemed much more than a temporary reassurance. It was a secret, ecstatic image, visible to Keelie's eyes alone, and it told her not to worry ever again; but the moment she realized this, unnerving anxiety followed. The image had gone away. Would it ever come back and confirm its secret? The next two nights, as if to tide Keelie over a difficult period without raising her hopes too high, Lora consented to appear, but for less than a second, not as close and slightly out of focus. Half in shadow, she stood on the balcony of her bedroom. She came up to a window only to close a shutter immediately. There was no way to decipher the expression on her face, everything seemed over before it started, and when Keelie opened her eyes again the room struck her as wretchedly small and dark, the night outside heavy with absence. These half glimpses, like tantalizing old snapshots, were still enough to let her sleep, but when she woke in the morning the sky looked tired. The more she allowed that one perfect appearance of Lora to haunt her, the harder it became to remember exactly how she looked. Like those that followed it went out of focus, blurred by separation. She even began to doubt that it had been as wonderful and complete as she'd thought.

There was no way of knowing now, because Lora wouldn't come back at all. Perhaps she'd really meant something quite different, not *Don't ever worry again,* but *Don't expect too much.* A week later, during the night, a storm came. The old elm overhanging the driveway was uprooted by the gale and crashed to the roof of a house below. After the shock, Keelie felt vaguely excited. The agent would have to write to Lora about it, and maybe this time there would be an answer. "When anything unexpected happens now, I start looking for . . ." But no answer came, and the agent merely pocketed the rent money until he'd covered the expense of clearing away the tree.

Her employer was out when Gary wandered into The Rummage Sale, rather stoned, to ask how much they'd give him for a Cardin suit. Keelie explained that it wasn't the kind of thing her customers went for and recommended a used-clothing store a few blocks away. "I'm too hungry to try anywhere right now," Gary said. "Will you buy me lunch?" She was surprised and attracted enough to stand him a double cheeseburger and apple pie à la mode. He told her about having recently returned from Japan and kissed her goodby on the mouth. She didn't really expect to see him again, but he reappeared at closing time, saying he'd changed his mind about the suit and would try to hang on to it until his luck changed. She found herself agreeing to let him ride her motorcycle back to his place in the hills. He set off at a pace that terrified her; she clung to his back and kept her eyes closed. Later he suggested they go out for ice cream, and when she refused he picked up her purse, took out a dollar bill and her key ring, and roared off again on her machine. Keelie remained lying naked on the mattress in the little shack, wondering whether in Gary's opinion his luck had changed and answered to her name. A few days later, however, she lent him fifteen dollars.

"Did Lora ever put in an appearance while you were with Gary?"

"No, she didn't bother, so I knew we'd never get anywhere much. Of course," Keelie corrected herself, "I knew that anyway."

We must have been standing on the balcony for more than half an hour while she talked. The light had slipped away like a discreet guest leaving a party who doesn't want his absence to be noticed. Now, suddenly, we missed it. She gave a little shiver and said, "Jesus, isn't it kind of cold?" Behind us, in the room, nobody seemed to have moved. It was dark in there, you could see only outlines of people. Sitar music played on the phonograph.

"Don't ask me to explain this. It's not difficult, it's impossible. Although I hope . . ." She stopped, apparently having forgotten what she hoped. "I had this beautiful time with Luke and Jim, two fantastic guys, but I couldn't live with their lives. You know? I didn't want to go out and get involved with changing things, and I didn't want to go off some place where it was supposed to be happy and peaceful. Everything sort of left me nowhere. And now, nothing—Luke, Jim, you standing right here so I can touch you, that music playing so I can hear it—nothing's as real to me as she is. And she's not even real. So how can that be, and what does it make me?"

As I parked outside the lodge, Keelie was waiting at the door, herself more like a visitant than a real person, barefoot, in black leather, hair flowing straight to her shoulders, heavy Indian rings of turquoise and silver flashing from her fingers as she waved. The driveway continued to the main house, a "Mediterranean" villa with arched windows, white stucco walls and a red-tiled roof. You could tell at a glance it was empty and the faded blinds across the windows had not been lowered yesterday or the day before; but there were surprisingly few signs of neglect. The lawns that sloped away on each side of the private road were rich and immaculate, beds of massed cinerarias had been freshly watered, spring roses bloomed and little trees of life, their leaves flecked with gold, grew erect from tubs on each side of the front door. I found the kind of total abandonment I'd expected only to the side of the house. An archway led to the patio, and beyond it the empty pool gaped like a question mark.

"Want to see inside?"

"Why not?"

I followed Keelie around the other side, to the kitchen window. She picked up a stone and calmly smashed a pane of glass. "Those terrible hooligans," she said. "Why do people do things like that? I tell the agent he really ought to have the property patroled."

The blinds over the living room windows wrapped everything in a half-light. Keelie pressed a switch and a naked bulb, hanging from the ceiling where there'd once been a chandelier, illuminated only more emptiness. I could see why she'd been disappointed. It felt like a place without secrets, scrupulously vacant. At one end was a built-in bar with a counter about five feet long. Somebody had scratched on it with a penknife, LEE SCREWED ANNIE HERE.

"Tricky," I said.

"Maybe it's a kick." Keelie shrugged. "People really do break in sometimes and that's usually the reason. A couple of times, when I've broken in, I could smell it."

"So you look around here quite often?"

She nodded. "I always kind of hope I might . . . But there's nothing. Never anything."

Upstairs, in the master bedroom, a wall mirror reflected another patch of emptiness where the bed had stood. The headboard had left a faint outline of itself on the wall. French windows opened to a little balcony with bougainvillea trailing across it. Below lay the patio and the pool with a crack across the middle.

Keelie opened a medicine cabinet in the bathroom and took out the cosmetic jar. The make-up had turned almost black with age and felt like stone.

"The only trick of the trade she left behind," I said.

Footfalls pattered across the roof.

"Squirrels," Keelie said. "Always playing."

At the lodge, her narrow, rather dingy living room bore traces of both Luke and Jim. A blown-up photograph of Che Guevara on one wall faced an Arlo Guthrie poster pinned to another. A transistor radio stood on a table next to a vase of roses. They were a pale orchid color, like the ones outside the house.

"I've got some low-calorie cola but it's full of cyclamates and I really ought to throw it out. How about freeze-dried coffee or instant tea?"

"Coffee's fine," I said, and asked if Lora had appeared again since we met. Keelie was standing in the kitchen doorway, hair falling over her face. She brushed it away and I saw the hopeful, anxious tremor in her eyes.

"Two nights ago I was just going to sleep. She seemed to be standing in a garden, above the ocean. She gave me a nice little nod, like I'd done something right. I'd called you that afternoon and asked you over. You think maybe she approves of you?"

I didn't answer.

"Or you think I'm crazy to even ask a question like that?" Keelie sat down on the arm of an imitation-leather chair. Like most of her gestures, it seemed temporary. She perched, she didn't sit, and wherever she was standing she wouldn't be there long. She picked one rose from the vase and sniffed it. "You're the only person I've met who knows anything about her. So can't you . . . ?" She broke off, put the rose back in the vase and disappeared into the kitchen.

I stared at the wall of ivy outside the windows. "As they say in show business, let's take it from the top. One thing is obvious. You were sitting on the beach when you first saw her, then you opened your eyes and saw Luke. He lived here. That's a connection."

"Yes, I worked that out too." Keelie returned from the kitchen with a chipped mug of tepid coffee. "But why didn't Luke ever see her?"

"From what you've told me, he doesn't sound the type."

She blinked with astonishment. "I'm the type?"

"It looks like it."

"But I'm a kind of nothing type," she said rather disarmingly. "I mean, who am I?"

"You're very open. Receptive. And you've got time to spare." I smiled at her. "It's more likely she'd want to get through to someone like you." A thought occurred. "If she *wants* to get through at all, of course."

Keelie blinked again. "You trying to tell me I could see her even if she didn't want me to?"

"I don't know. Maybe. Just because somebody is *there,* you can't assume they want to be there. Or want you to see them there."

"Now you've really complicated it. I think I'm more confused than ever." She sat on the arm of the chair again, jumped up after a moment. "But if it started with her not wanting to be seen, and me not wanting to see her—how could it ever get started?"

"Maybe you were just getting a message, receiving something because you happened to be in the right place."

"Like bird shit?" She giggled suddenly, then began walking up and down the little room, from Che to Arlo. "But that's scary. I could get all kinds of messages I didn't want."

"We all do."

Stopping, she gave me an uncertain, apprehensive look.

"You got the dead man in his car. Didn't want him, did you?"

"I hope not." She frowned. "I don't think so. But I wish you hadn't said that. Don't forget you're talking to someone who's not all that bright. She can believe any-thing . . ." Keelie perched on the chair again, crossed her arms, gave herself a little hug. "I asked my mother once how people can look at the same thing you're looking at but see something quite different. She couldn't explain.

She said it had never happened to her, and not to believe everything you see, anyway." Keelie's eyelids drooped and her mouth became almost voluptuous. She seemed to be wrapping herself in her mystery, adoring it like the child who prefers giants and witches to uncles and aunts. "Let's do a joint, want to do a joint?" I told her to go ahead and she said, "No, you too. We'll get beautifully relaxed, then maybe . . . Goddamit, she certainly *ought* to let you see her too."

"Like a seance? I'm sure it doesn't work that way. She never seems to arrive when you expect her." But Keelie looked so disappointed that I said, "Okay, we can try."

In the silence, in the corridorlike room, we started the joint. I seldom smoke pot, too often it gives me a low rather than a high and makes me want to go home. Keelie took her first, long, eager drag with a confident smile, as if welcoming an old friend, and I rather envied her. She switched on the transistor radio. It was tuned to the classical-music station. Absurdly incongruous baroque music played very loud, making the room seem smaller than ever. We listened to it, passing the joint back and forth, then she switched the radio off and lay on the narrow couch, on her back, hands folded across her breasts.

She remained there, still at last, on the way to her other place. You could hardly tell that she was breathing. I thought, Of all the people with a hunger for somewhere else, not really believing the world into which they were born, just rooming there, she seems to want to go the farthest away. Then I closed my eyes and heard the sound of a plane very high in the sky. When I looked up again, Keelie was perched on the arm of the chair, watching me.

"Nothing?"

"Nothing."

She asked with a sigh, "Do you think she's my enemy or my friend?"

"There's no reason to suppose she doesn't mean well. I'd say that she's your friend."

Keelie nodded and gazed rather blankly at the room, taking in her little cell of reality. "I hope so. I could certainly use one."

A few evenings later I'm looking at a photograph of Keelie's friend. At the movie bookstore I found two antique issues of a movie magazine called *ScreenTime,* each containing an interview with Lora Chase. In the first, it is 1942 and she wears dark satin pajamas. The photograph shows only a corner of the living room that I know as bare and twilit, but the white couch on which she sits implies the kind of airy luxury that she so often enjoyed in her movies. She is talking about Love. The reporter asks why she never married, and she tells him, "Ten years under contract to a studio gave me a deep distaste for signing myself away to anyone or anything." Her legs are crossed and her beautiful, searching eyes gaze directly at the camera and revive the old impression that she's really looking at something far away.

The second photograph is taken ten years later, and she talks "frankly" about her life in the meantime, the alcoholism and the conversion to the Catholic Church. She sits on the same couch and her legs are crossed, and although she wears a rather severe blouse and skirt and her hair is shorter, she seems no older. It might be a test shot for another part. "I didn't start drinking because I lost a man or a role," she tells the reporter. "It was nothing ridiculous like that. I suppose it was some kind of escape." The reporter asks what she was escaping from, and she says, "Myself, I suppose. Don't we all try to escape from ourselves?" Her eyes gaze out, direct and candid as before. "But why don't you ask me what I was escaping *to*?" The reporter obliges. "Well, when I was really quite far gone, I met a wonderful man called Father Wentworth. He said that people escape to God by the most unexpected routes, and maybe drinking was mine."

I wonder how Father Wentworth reacted when she left the arms of the Church for those of General Alberti. Anyway, there is no chink of reality admitted here; you don't expect it in the interviews, of course, but the face gives nothing away beyond an infinite, perfect readiness for the camera. You can spray a chemical on the fabric of chairs and couches that creates an invisible film, refusing all marks and stains, protecting it even from excrement and blood. She must have a similar preparation for herself, she looks so sublimely remote from *ScreenTime,* drinking and God.

The phone rings. "Quick, turn on the news on Channel Four!" Keelie sounds out of breath. Behind her I can hear a murmur of voices. "Tell me if you see who I think I see, and don't hang up, I'm not home, I'm at a friend's place!"

I switch on the TV and, from the sound that precedes the image, learn that I'm at Kennedy Airport. Passengers on a flight from New York to Mexico City that was hijacked to Cuba have just been brought back, after an overnight stay in Havana. The first image that appears on the screen is of an elderly Jew, or perhaps not so elderly, no older than Lora, but his face as cratered by anxiety as hers is smooth and free. He speaks with a kind of weary international-refugee accent that suggests an endless moving from place to place. He tells the TV reporter that he wasn't particularly frightened, he experienced far worse things under the Nazis. He praises the pilot and the stewardesses. Then a stewardess praises the pilot. Nobody has any impressions of Havana. They were all confined to a hotel and treated pleasantly, although the service was poor.

Then, in a shot that shows more of the passengers, I notice a woman sitting by herself on a bench in the background. She's half turned away from the camera, having no part of it, no intention of discussing her feelings or her night in Havana, waiting to be allowed to proceed through customs and disappear. She wears a red pants suit and a straw hat. Her legs are crossed. A man walks past, blotting her from sight. When he's gone, she begins to turn toward the camera, as if looking for something, but the image is abruptly cut off and a pain-killer commercial takes over. There has been just enough time to decide that she could be Lora Chase, then that she's not, before I never see her again.

"I don't know," I tell Keelie. "Was there more of her, closer?"

"Not closer, just more. But I really believe it was her, it was Lora, even though I'm kind of stoned. They just turned on the news here, you know, I wasn't paying any attention, I never look at stuff like that, then suddenly, before I even saw her, I got these *goose pimples* . . . And she used to live in Mexico City, remember, so it all begins to add up, I mean she might be going back. Suppose I call the airline and pretend I'm her sister and worried to death, will they read me the passenger list?"

"It's worth a try. Of course, they won't give you her address or anything."

"I know. But to see her alive and real! Only on TV, of course, but really *there*. It's . . ." She trails off. There's a burst of laughter in the room behind her.

"If you don't get anywhere with the airline, I'll give you a consolation prize," I tell her and explain about the magazines and the interviews.

"Oh, fantastic! Are they . . . ? Does she . . . ?"

"Not really. No matter what she seems to be saying, she's not saying anything at all."

"I don't believe it!" Keelie sounds shocked and goes on to explain that it doesn't make sense for one person to make such claims on another's attention without having something important to say.

She opened the door of the lodge and was not exactly the same person. There was no physical change, nothing in her face to suggest a new happiness or unhappiness. Whatever had occurred was more like a variation in the light around her, like the difference between seeing the same room or landscape in the morning and the late afternoon. I remembered a comment the director had made about Lora: "You never got close." This was how it felt with Keelie today. She had crossed a line, stepping over into the same kind of atmosphere that enveloped Lora Chase on the screen, she looked at and past me, to something beyond, and however near to me she stood, the impression persisted that she was out of reach.

The airline official had told her there was no one on the plane called Lora Chase, but it didn't shake her at all. "How does *he* know? She could have gotten married. Or maybe it's not her real name." (But according to the reference books, it is.) "There's a hundred different reasons why he didn't know." She sat on the edge of the couch, thumbnail between her teeth. "Still, I think it's kind of mean of *her* not to give me a sign. Couldn't she just appear and nod her head or something? I haven't seen her at all in over two weeks." There was a new, intimate tone of complaint, as if their relationship had changed simply because she believed she'd seen Lora on the TV screen. In some way it made her more "real." She was becoming possessive toward her possessor now that she felt a part of the mystery had lifted. It hadn't, of course, but the only way to follow Keelie's experience was to see that it made its own laws.

The room had a terribly solitary air, not just because it was small and plain; there was nothing of her own in it, only the kind of furniture nobody except a landlord buys, and the posters that had never been hers. "When I was at school I had this girlfriend who wrote to Ava Gardner . . ." She gave me a quick, oblique glance, then got up suddenly. "She thought Ava was the most beautiful person in the world, and she felt sorry for her too, she couldn't explain why. It was the message she got from watching her up there. So she wrote this long letter and poured out her heart and Ava never answered. And my girlfriend really turned against her. Whenever she read bad news about her— another divorce, or she'd broken up with somebody—she'd say, 'Well, she's that kind of person, that's how she is, some people are their own worst enemies.' I thought maybe Ava just never got that letter, but my girlfriend was convinced she had." Another glance. "You think now I'm behaving like she did?"

"Not really. It's more complicated. You never poured out your heart—"

"Oh, but I did!" Her eyes glistened. "I never wrote her, of course, but you've no idea what I . . ." She turned abruptly away from me, stared out at the dark wall of ivy. "What *is* it about actors? I mean, who *are* they? They can be so beautiful in something, and so mean in something else, and it's never what they really are. Is it . . . ? Maybe even if you went to bed with one, you'd feel you were being made love to by a mask. And Lora—" she created a little pause, a hush, around the name—"even though I've never seen her act, she's like all of them that ever lived, all in one person. That one time, in the night, she was so *completely* . . ."

"What?"

"Anything—everything—you can possibly imagine."

She was so certain, I felt clumsy for asking questions. "But how can you know? You've forgotten what she looked like."

"If someone looked at you that way, you'd remember it even though you'd forgotten it." She walked to the window on the other side of the room and stood gazing out toward the house.

"Then whatever she did that night, it was her greatest performance."

"Right. If I saw her in a movie now, it could only be a let-down." Keelie continued to stare out of the window. The gardener was working outside the house, sprinklers played on the lawns. "He never met her," she said absently. "I asked, but he's just another one who never met her. Listen, when we were talking here last time and you said, 'Let's take it from the top,' you didn't really."

"How was that?"

"It started before Luke. Why did I walk out on my family that particular day? Why not the day before or the day after? Nothing special happened that day. And why did I get a ride from someone who dropped me off right opposite that beach? It's pretty clear to me this whole thing had been waiting a long time to happen."

"I agree."

"Really?" She gave me a thoughtful look. "I think I believe you. I can't talk about her with anyone else this way. After the first time, I never mentioned it to Luke, because he didn't seem to react. And I never told Jim. I started to tell my best girlfriend, but she . . ." Biting her thumbnail, Keelie scrutinized me again. "You're not just pretending to go along with it because you don't want to tell me you think I'm a nut?"

I shook my head.

"I think I believe you. Why do you believe me?"

"You're more believable than any kind of explanation."

She looked delighted as a child who's been acquitted of lying.

"Anything else would be psychoanalysis," I said.

"And you don't go along with that?"

"Jung told a good story on himself. A woman came to see him, she seemed perfectly normal, but she insisted that whenever she went out of doors, birds flew out of the sky and attacked her. So Jung attacked this interesting problem of why this apparently happy, well-adjusted person should have this crazy delusion, and she came to see him twice a week for two years, and they went into everything, and in the end he found the reason and explained it to her and told her she was cured. She was terribly relieved and grateful, and he showed her to the door, and she went out and birds came down from the sky and attacked her."

"Oh, beautiful. You see, if I don't believe myself, I'm a nut. Now let me ask you something else. People give out that line about great people and ideas *living on* in books. Why can't acting live on, too? Can all that acting, all those parts, just go away?"

"Yes. Once it's over, it doesn't exist any more. You can only imagine it does."

"Then it does." She laughed. "Because I imagine it. And who does reality *belong* to, anyway? Why are people so mean about it, telling you no, you can't have *that* piece, it's not real . . . ?" Keelie turned back to the window. "My family always did that, kept saying I had to get my feet on the ground. Well, maybe *some* ground, but not theirs . . ." She began slowly drawing down the shade. "It's different for you, a writer can make someone like Lora into a character and get rid of her if he wants, but all I can do is . . ." The lowered shade cut off the view of the house. The sun came from that side and the light in the room grew overcast. It seemed to change her mood. She spoke half to herself, in a doubtful, pleading voice. "Maybe it's *my* fault recently. Maybe she's staying away because I'm not doing something right."

I thought of the boy in the cemetery, laying three roses on the star's grave, and it seemed so simple, so unmysterious, she was dead and he mourned her, which solved everything for him. If Keelie read in the papers tomorrow that Lora Chase had died a few months ago, it might even be over for both of them, an open-and-shut case of one person unable, for the best of reasons, to reach another.

Still standing by the shaded window, she clung to herself in the way I'd seen before, wrapping herself in her mystery, secure inside it. "The birds came down from the sky and attacked her," she said. "You've no idea how good that makes me feel."

We had arranged to meet outside the studio gate. Keelie rode up on her motorcycle and parked it on the lot between a Mercedes and a Rolls. The cop checked my pass; we walked along an alley with closed faceless buildings, then past the entrance to the permanent exterior Western set, as still and abandoned as the offices. Dust seemed to have settled there a long time ago. A sudden view of some outlying Hollywood suburbs on the rise of a hill looked rather unconvincing, like a backdrop. Another, thinner alley between more buildings led past doors marked 101, 103, 105. There was no sound except our footsteps. Years ago, Lora Chase had made several movies at this studio, and Keelie glanced at each locked door and blinded window as if they might contain some sign. There was none, of course. Closed down, the studio had become simply a disused factory. In a few months it would probably open again, when another bank or petroleum company came to the rescue, but in the meantime it was about to auction off its past. Like worlds being broken up, the furniture, costumes, rugs, props and decorations from a thousand movies were due for the block. Perhaps this impending auction frightened away the ghosts. No place could feel less haunted. Keelie said that it reminded her of Lora's house.

The great windowless sound stages stretched away like tombs. Outside one of them stood a portable dressing room. The door had slipped its latch. Inside, an empty couch faced an empty chair, and the dressing-table mirror reflected Keelie's anxious, peering face. It felt for a moment like a scene from a Western, the covered wagon abandoned by pioneers. You expected whooping Indians to descend upon it.

A sign with a black arrow aimed at a stage with "17" painted in black letters on the side. A cop at the door checked my second pass—for the auction preview. Entering, we were confronted by a gigantic collection of places and things, overpowering and outnumbering the people who moved slowly, carefully around them. There were complete rooms arranged like sets and separate displays of all kinds of objects, harps, sarcophagi, gas chandeliers, bird cages, suits of armor, marble columns surmounted by Winged Victories. It was like coming upon the site of an ancient civilization, weirdly immaculate in spite of time, except that these were all relics of a civilization that had never existed, borrowed for a world of pretending, not living. I saw a matron in a pants suit, obviously wealthy from the back, in a nineteenth-century Russian drawing room overhung with gloom and piety. She examined ikon-like portraits, plaster-cast angels on pedestals with their hands folded in prayer, a gleaming but empty samovar. In the same period, but in a different country, a young couple wearing sweaters and Levis stood in a beautifully cluttered London room, surrounded by overstuffed chairs with backs shaped like balloons, dark antique cabinets and clocks heavy and elaborate enough to slow down time. An actress I recognized in spite or because of her huge dark glasses sat on a canopied fourposter with misty curtains and unlit candelabra emerging from its pillars. And an old man, very correctly dressed, presided alone in a throne chair at the head of a banqueting table long enough to seat thirty on each side.

Keelie gave me a look that said, "You think *I* imagine things?" Earlier, she'd asked me to point out at once anything I thought I recognized from one of Lora's movies, a chair on which she might have sat, a portrait underneath which she might have stood. She seemed to forget about this now as she stepped from movie to movie, finally sitting down on a backless Egyptian-style sofa with hieroglyphics and sphinxes carved on the arms. Besides, I didn't find anything. I had never seen Lora in a costume film, and all the white couches and easy chairs, the beds with satin headboards and elegant wicker furniture that evoked affluent verandas at twilight were hard to tell one from the other. Almost certainly she had wakened up in one of those beds, met a lover at night on one of those verandas, paused to smile at herself in one of the many antiqued, gilt-framed mirrors, but it was impossible to be sure.

The matron with a wealthy back suddenly appeared, coming toward us now. It was Juliet Kappler. She told me on it. I introduced her to Keelie, who said very politely, she'd found an exceptional Tiffany lamp and placed a bid. "Hello, nice to meet you." Juliet raised an eyebrow at her black leather, then sat on the opposite end of the sofa. I asked after Paul and Lilian. They were both absolutely fine. We lit cigarettes, and a guard hurried over, ordering us to put them out. "Rather absurd," Juliet said calmly. "In one sense, it's all gone up in smoke already."

A thought occurred. Her husband had been an agent and a producer. I asked Juliet if she'd ever known Lora Chase. She leaned back, as if in the direction of memory, then realized the sofa was backless. "Of course I *met* her," she said. "But I haven't seen her in years. Has anyone?"

Keelie gave a little gasp. "What was she like?"

"Falling-down drunk, usually." Juliet sounded matter-of-fact and not very interested.

"You saw that? You saw her drunk somewhere?"

"Oh yes. At two or three parties. Then people stopped asking her, of course. It was embarrassing."

Keelie said, "Excuse me, what was she like, drunk?"

"Boring, with a tendency to baby talk." Juliet sighed. "Then she found God and got it together again, I believe." She looked from Keelie to myself in airy surprise. "Now why this interest in Lora Chase, of all people?"

Secretive, very still, Keelie pressed her lips together.

"I always liked her as an actress," I said.

"Really? I must say, she never . . ." Something in Juliet's tone shook Keelie out of her secrecy. Her eyelids fluttered as if she expected a blow. Aware of this, Juliet gave a reassuring smile. "But she was always quite beautiful, I realize that." She glanced at her watch and got up.

Keelie said, "And did you ever go to her house?"

"The one she used to have, somewhere in the hills?"

"Right! She still has it. I mean, she never sold it."

"Yes, we were there once, I remember. When Marty— my husband—was still an agent and we were still married, she wanted him to handle her. She took the social route, asked us to dinner. She wasn't drinking then, of course, but it didn't work out because Marty never felt she had quite enough style. He was always choosy." A large funeral urn beside the sofa caught Juliet's eye. She ran her hand over the frieze. "There were so many like that. Beautiful, not untalented, but not quite . . ." She wondered if the urn would make a good lamp base, decided it might look morbid, kissed me lightly, nodded to Keelie and vanished into the room of Victorian clutter, behind a giant embroidered fire screen.

Staring after her, Keelie blew a mild raspberry at her back. "I'm sorry if she's a friend of yours. And listen, would you please go away? Just for a little while? I want to be here by myself."

The secretive look had returned to her face. Her hands with Indian rings on the fingers were so tightly clasped together that the knuckles had gone pale.

"Are you all right, Keelie?"

"I'm fine, why shouldn't I be?" She brushed away a long strand of hair, but it fell back, almost masking her eyes.

I wandered off, past the huge banquet table at which people were now seated in separate groups, talking very quietly as if in church. Perhaps in some after-dinner fantasy, the old man leaned back in his throne chair, eyes closed. Beyond this was an unexpected enclave of stuffed animals, owls and stags' heads with polished antlers and beady artificial eyes. Stepping through a bead curtain, I reached somewhere in the Far East, lacquered chests, a row of miniature pagodas, a table in the shape of a lotus flower. The guard came up behind me. "Excuse me, sir, your young lady doesn't seem to be feeling well." I followed him back and there was no one where I'd left Keelie, just the empty sofa, an array of little golden chairs with more sphinxes on their arms, and the funeral urn.

The guard led me around to the other side of the sofa. Keelie knelt on the floor, head between her knees. "It's okay . . ." Her voice sounded muffled but firm. "Just wait till the blood gets back to my brain." After about a minute she got to her feet, refusing my help. Her cheeks were flushed. She looked away sharply, toward the far end of the stage, gave a little moan of disappointment and sat on the sofa. Slowly, she passed one hand over her forehead and face. "Jesus, I'm so hot. A moment ago I was so cold." She looked away again, in the same direction as before.

Against one wall with EXIT painted on it stood a large and uncompromisingly white example of *moderne* furniture, a circular divan from the center of which rose a kind of thin upholstered pillar. Focused nearby was one of those pole lamps that imitate a movie spotlight. The fashion evoked was from films of thirty or more years ago, a scene in an expensive apartment with a view of the Manhattan skyline (there would have been a grand piano, too); austerely sophisticated in its time, the style had been *déclassé* for years. Now a relic in its unimportant corner, the divan was a thing without atmosphere, sterile and bleak.

"She was sitting on it by herself," Keelie said. "I hadn't even closed my eyes."

"What was she doing?"

"Nothing. She never looked at me, she didn't notice me."

"What was she wearing?"

"Black. And she seemed younger than before. It was like looking at an old movie, everything black and white. But so quick! There was hardly time to . . ."

"You saw her, and then she vanished?"

"Not exactly. It began with this really shaky feeling. I mean, so different from the other times because I never closed my eyes and she never looked at me. I thought I was going to pass out, so I put my head between my legs."

"And she'd gone when you looked up again?"

"Right." Keelie stood up. "I'm okay now, let's go over."

Cushions fanned out from the center of the divan, making it look like an inverted umbrella. The spotlight gleamed on its whiteness. One of the cushions was slightly sunken, as if someone had recently sat there. Keelie laughed and sat there too. "Okay, Lora, where are you? Put up or shut up. It's getting too much." Then, in a childish singsong voice: "Go away, never come back, push off, get lost, drop dead . . ." She kicked the base of the lamp, turning its light from her face. "I wish I knew a spell or something. What do they call it?"

"Exorcism. But that's for ghosts."

"Goddamit. So what is *she*?"

Not long ago, astronomers began sighting dim objects that reeled across the sky, so far away in space and time that their light must originally have been produced millions of years before and took eons to become visible from the earth. Fragments of a remote past, they still had enough energy left to travel almost as fast as light. So if the universe was created by some immense cosmic explosion, beginning rather than ending with a bang, these lonely specks that resemble stars, quasi-stellar objects being their official name, are the last remnants of that first creation.

"What are you thinking about?" Keelie asked, staring at me.

There seemed to be a connection, but too difficult to explain. "A woman was recently woken up in the middle of the night," I said, "by the sound of some deafeningly loud music from a brass band. There was no radio playing in the house, and anyway the sound seemed to be coming from her mouth. It turned out the fillings in her teeth, combined with the acid in her saliva, had formed a receiving system. She was picking up sound waves from a loudspeaker phonograph being played down the street."

"Wow." Then she giggled. "But I couldn't pick up Lora Chase that way. I mean, my teeth are perfect. Never had a filling in my life."

We walked back through the empty silent alleys, Keelie hurrying ahead with her eyes fixed on the ground.

"You look as if you *don't* want to see her now," I said.

"Right. If she's going to show up when my eyes are open, and she does it now, and *you* don't see her too, I'll feel such a . . ." At the parking lot she gave a sigh of relief. "All the same, my head is still where it wants to be. I didn't mean it about wanting her to go away. If she went away now, the rest of my life would be completely impossible. I'd never know *why*."

She put on her crash helmet, revved up the engine and zoomed into the boulevard, disappearing quickly among traffic, billboards and palm trees.

•

She disappears for some time after this; our tenuous connection, which depends on somebody that neither of us has ever met, slips away to a talk on the phone about once a week. I suppose we've both agreed that there's no reason to see each other again until something happens. That room at the lodge grows smaller in my mind. Occasionally I imagine her standing there to watch the gardener, or hurrying up the driveway to break the kitchen window again. More leaves drip into the empty swimming pool. She picks some fresh roses. Her head is still where it wants to be.

On my work table, along with untidy piles of typescripts, letters, notes to myself, newspaper and magazine cuttings, there's a folder marked LORA CHASE. After a phone call from Keelie, I make a note of what she says. The words on these pieces of paper read like telegraphic dispatches from the front of her life.

"More of them screwing in the house. I'm getting a bit fed up with it."

"Yesterday, just getting home from work. I looked up the driveway and she's outside the front door again. Doesn't see me. I actually call out and she turns away and goes inside."

"Lost my job. But they tell me I've made just enough to qualify for unemployment and you can live on the minimum for a while."

"I couldn't be more broke and she turns up wearing a fantastic gown, with diamonds. Walks across the lawn and through the wall."

"I met this guy I kind of like, so he's moving in. His name—are you ready?—is *Gordon*. He does a lot of different things, like he's a masseur and a window designer and a Virgo and speaks perfect Spanish, but he's broke too."

"The third week she hasn't been near me. Gordon can't understand why I'm so nervous, but I'm not telling him anything."

"At a Love-In. We both got completely stoned, but in a crowd like that I couldn't miss anyone like her. Lying on the grass on a blanket, with a picnic basket, taking sun like it was the beach."

"It's been *five* weeks this time!"

"So finally she turns up, at the worst possible moment. Comes into the bedroom while Gordon is screwing me. I jump up, go to the kitchen and make coffee."

"No, he moved out."

"Just sitting by myself, listening to the radio. And there she is *in the doorway,* with a kind of 'may I come in?' expression on her face. Then she *sees* me for the first time in months, looks as if she's come to the wrong place and it's awful, goes right out again. Or maybe I dreamed this?"

"I know it sounds crazy but I woke up in the middle of the night and *knew* there were people screwing again in the house. Got up and went to the driveway and there was a car parked right outside the gates. I think I heard them go away later."

"Got a job. Bottomless dancer, no kidding, some club out in the Valley. I can't dance but it doesn't matter. They like my ass."

"Can't remember when she made me feel so good. I was pretty tired, after two o'clock in the morning, and I came out to the parking lot and there was a limousine next to my bike. Chauffeur at the wheel, everything very grand.

The back window rolls down and she leans out, smiles and waves at me, then the limousine drives off."

"You know something? I could do okay as a hooker. You probably know that's what most of these places are about. But it's not my kind of thing. Johns make me laugh."

"No, not in a couple of weeks."

"They didn't fire me, they just went broke. But you can live on the minimum for a while."

"You ever get that feeling? Everything kind of blah?"

"Nice of you to call. No, nothing's wrong. Or right. Let's see . . . Six weeks, maybe seven."

"I'm beginning to worry that something's happened to her. Or to *me* . . ."

Another month passed. I heard nothing from her, called twice and both times got no answer. The third time, the phone was lifted off the hook and that was all. A few days later, after lunching in Hollywood with a producer who wanted to film *Steppenwolf* (they happen, like really heavy rains, about once every three years), I drove up to the house in the hills. Two empty garbage cans stood outside the gates. I parked, went up to the lodge, noticing the motorcycle near the front door and the gardens vibrant with roses. Nobody answered the bell, but the door was off the latch. In the living room, shades were drawn over the windows and the half-lit air felt heavy and stale. Unwashed dishes were scattered about the kitchen. The shades were drawn in the bedroom too, but I could see Keelie on the bed, apparently asleep. She was wrapped in a white bathrobe that looked much too big for her; it covered her ankles and was presumably a legacy from Luke or Jim or Gordon.

When I called her name she woke with a violent, electrifying start, sitting upright, her mouth open in a silent cry. Then: "Oh, it's you," she said. "I thought . . ." She lay down again and remained perfectly still.

"What's up?"

"I'm down." She turned on her side.

I started to raise one of the shades, and she protested. It was too bright outside. I began to feel, as she had done when Lora appeared on the sound stage, that I'd stepped into a world of black and white, like an old movie: the half-light, the blown-up photographs and dark furniture in the living room, the white sheets and robe and face on the bed. And her eyes, I remembered, were gray.

I drew up a shade part of the way and she flung an arm across her face. "Please, I'm not used to it."

"You haven't been out recently?"

"No, I've been staying home."

"Shall I make some coffee?"

She shook her head, then got up, arm still shielding her face, and walked without a word to the kitchen. Opening the refrigerator, she took out a flagon of cheap California wine and filled a tooth glass to the brim. "Help yourself if you want." I only wanted to open a window and started to draw up one of the living-room shades. She blinked. "Jesus, please, no health routine." She sat on the arm of a chair, and before she turned her face away from the light I saw her red-rimmed eyes. Her feet were filthy, too. "The scene speaks for itself," she said, and drank some wine.

"How long since you saw her?"

"Three months." Her voice was resentful. "Why did you come?"

"I had a feeling something was up."

"Down."

"Yes, you look awful."

"Thanks." She got up, lowered the shade, walked back to the kitchen to refill her glass. "My best girlfriend dropped by a couple of weeks ago and thought I was going crazy. But I wouldn't explain anything." She came back as far as the doorway. "She made such a thing about it, though, I finally let her drive me to the Free Clinic. She said it was fantastic, she'd gone there herself for gonorrhea shots and they had psychiatrists too. I waited around with a lot of girls who looked like their babies were going to burst out any minute."

The psychiatrist had a patient middle-aged smile and she knew at once there was no possibility of contact. It seemed hopeless to try and tell him anything, but ridiculous not to, having waited all that time. He listened without visible surprise, nodded once or twice, scribbled some notes, then explained that she had an identity crisis. Many young people who came to consult him were suffering from this crisis. She wanted to know exactly what it was, and he said, "It means you don't know who you are." Keelie giggled suddenly. "But suppose I'm nobody?" The psychiatrist told her that everybody has to be somebody. Many of his patients, he said, had chosen drugs as a way of escaping from the crisis, and he was tempted to classify Lora as Keelie's drug. She was clearly addicted and undergoing enforced withdrawal symptoms before his eyes. The important thing was for Keelie to realize that she didn't need Lora, she only thought she did. Next time, they'd start exploring *why*. He made another appointment for her, sent her to the next room for vitamin shots, and her girlfriend drove her back to the lodge. "I haven't been out since. I guess she's given me up."

"And you had enough food in the house not to go out again?"

She shook her head. "I order wine from the liquor store down the hill and they send up potato chips as well." She walked past me, toward the bedroom. "I'm sorry, I don't feel like talking any more."

"How about taking a walk?"

She stopped, turning back to look rather suspiciously at me. "Why?"

"It's a beautiful day. You needn't talk any more, just look at it."

She stared at her wine. "Where?"

"Outside, in the gardens."

After a moment she shook her head.

"Come on. Or at least take a shower. Do something."

She shook her head again, then her face went completely blank. "I can't understand why such a thing could happen to anybody." She continued to the bedroom and closed the door.

The phone rang.

"You were trying to be friendly, I was trying to be unfriendly. I'm sorry." I heard a faint laugh. "But I'm okay now. I took a shower."

"Good."

"And it sort of went on from there."

"Have you been out?"

"No, but I started thinking. And I think I really know *why*. She wants me to leave, all along she's been warning me not to stay. And she ought to know. Look at what this town did to her—"

"You know what she wants even when she's not there?"

"What's the first thing that happens to me when I arrive in this town?" Keelie said obstinately. They always call it "this town" when they've decided to leave. "She comes out of nowhere, like out of the sea. She was warning me. And she's right, this town is dying, it's a place to die. I've got to get out."

"Where will you go?"

"I've thought about that too. I've got just enough money left for gas and whatever, so I'll ride to New Mexico and find Jim."

"You've heard from him? He's still there?"

"I don't know. But there's bound to be people there. And . . ." A sudden pause. "Could she follow me or is that ridiculous?"

"Ridiculous. You're not running away from her."

"But if she turned up there, it could be another warning. I don't want to be told I'm in the wrong place forever."

"Don't worry."

"No. And when I think about going to New Mexico, it feels like the right place. Free. *Away.* I want to close my eyes."

"Drop me a postcard, then."

"Okay. Goodby now."

•

The phone rang again.

"D'you have a moment?"

Her voice sounded very far away; I thought she must be already on the road.

"No, I'm still here. At the lodge. I just got back from settling with the agent about the rent, and you won't believe what happened."

"If you tell me, Keelie, I think I will."

"Are you ready? The birds came out of the sky! I just talked to Lora Chase, in person, over the phone. She's at the Beverly Hills Hotel."

"Since when?"

"The agent told me she flew in late last night. Isn't that something? I mean, she arrives just as I'm getting ready to leave. The agent doesn't know where she came *from*. He just got a telegram from her lawyer in New York yesterday, saying to expect her. She owns quite a bit of property around town as well as the house. He said a lot of the old-timers invested in property. And she's here to sell or buy, I don't remember which, anyway he's got business with her. So I called, and you can imagine."

"Not as well as you'll tell it."

I heard a sigh. "She was fantastic. I started in and thought I must be sounding like a complete idiot. 'Excuse me, Miss Chase, my name is Keelie Drake, and I rent the lodge at your old house, and I keep on seeing you.' And I rapped on, and after I'd told her about the first two or three times, I thought I'd better stop. All she said was, in a kind of marvelous voice, *'Go on.'* Just that. *'Go on.'* You remember her voice?"

"Perfectly pitched for lying."

"What?"

"Whenever she had to lie in a movie, she spoke the lines so beautifully."

"So I went on. And told her almost everything. Including how I'd missed her recently, and it made me . . . The really fantastic part is, she wants to see me."

I was convinced she'd gone over to the edge. "Maybe that's not a good idea. Wouldn't it be better just to—"

"Are you crazy? Let me tell you something else she said. She's so cool. 'Well,' she said, 'many years ago, a critic wrote about me in a film that I had magic. It seems I haven't lost it.'"

"She always had style, too. When are you going to see her?"

"This afternoon. She wants to come to the lodge. Will you . . . ?"

"Of course. I was hoping you'd invite me."

"Great. And . . ." A hesitation. "Even though she sounds so fantastic, I don't think I want to be alone with her."

"Why?"

"You'd never believe she was really here. And I'm kind of embarrassed I never saw any of her movies. Be sure to tell her how great you thought she used to be."

Doubting her existence in the flesh much more than in Keelie's mind, I stood at the window and saw a cab draw up outside the gates. A woman emerged into bright, perfect sunlight and clear air. She wore black. Walking toward the lodge, she stopped suddenly, like an animal sniffing prey. Alone, motionless, she gazed at the driveway and the house. Keelie came out from the lodge, barefoot, wearing a white shift. The woman didn't notice her at first. Then she turned. Keelie went very still. Time seemed to be holding its breath until Lora moved slowly toward her and held out her hand.

Entering the living room was like an entrance from one of her movies, except for the dreary little set. Her composure was too graceful and practiced not to conceal a mystery. Her midi-length dress could have been worn twenty years ago. I saw nothing as abstract as a figure: a body, still retaining its discreet sexuality. A trace of looseness in her movements suggested it had been much used, there was no touch or exploration it hadn't known. Just inside the doorway she hesitated, as if crossing the room were more than a short journey. She came closer, borne on a current of perfume, and the long dark hair was a wig and she smiled too carefully. Skin almost unlined, but stretched very tight over delicately firm bones. She must have had several lifts.

I wondered what Keelie thought about this. She gave no sign that she saw any difference between Lora as she'd appeared and Lora now in this room. For her the actual presence dazzled comparison, even though it wasn't in Lora's favor. The opposite for me. Seeing her get out of the cab, I was prepared for anything, even hoping for the inexplicable. Having gone this far, she could cross the time gap and preserve, as she had for Keelie, the figure I remembered. It lasted only a moment, before she moved across the room. Then she patted her wig and smiled too carefully again as we were introduced.

"He knows about this whole thing," Keelie said. "And he saw your movies when he was a kid."

A hand was held out toward me. It felt cool, very slightly moist. "And did you go to them by yourself?" Her voice sounded a little lower than it used to be, but still pliant and faintly mocking.

"Yes. You can tell?"

She nodded. "Your parents would never have taken you. I wasn't exactly family entertainment." She gave me a long, amused glance. "You sneaked off, then. To another world." I would have paid her a compliment if she'd given me time, but she didn't seem to want it. Turning back to Keelie: "This little place was just the servants' quarters when I lived in the house. I hope you're not paying too much rent."

"Ninety a month," Keelie said.

She considered this, quickly reconnoitering the kitchen and bedroom. "No, you're not. I'm glad."

Keelie asked if she'd like some coffee. She shook her head. "Some wine maybe? I think I've got some wine left." Another shake of the head. "I don't drink. Nothing, thank you." She gazed around the little room, as if wondering where to sit. Finally she settled on the couch, crossing her legs.

Keelie watched every movement. "You're comfortable there? Maybe the chair—"

"This is fine." She glanced at her watch. "I don't have a great deal of time. Shall we start talking about the important thing?"

Keelie blinked. Outside, everything was extraordinarily silent. "Did I make sense on the phone?" she said.

"Certainly." Palms together, her hands waited on her lap.

"Well . . . I told you—"

"I know what you told me." There was a shade of impatience in the voice. "First you could only see me when your eyes were closed. Then, apparently, I was there when your eyes were open."

"Right."

Fingers drummed lightly against each other. "Years ago, I had an idea of going on the stage. There was a play that appealed to me. But my agent talked me out of it, he said I lacked projection."

Keelie suddenly squatted on the floor at her feet.

The hands went still. "You must stop doing that."

"What?"

"Looking at me that way. As if I'm not real. Why do you think I've come to see you?"

"I'm sorry." Keelie's hair fell over her face. She brushed it away rather timidly. "Of course you wanted to show me you're real."

"Partly." There was a pause, and I heard the total silence outside again. "But only *partly*." She lingered over the word as if it amused her. "I'm also here because I *believe* you. Every word. I'm sure I was in all those places you saw me."

"Even with my eyes closed?"

"There's a place, I believe, called the mind's eye."

"Oh, fantastic. You're into all of that too?"

Lora glanced down at the eager face. I had the same feeling as in her movies, she wasn't really looking at Keelie at all. Perhaps, I thought suddenly, there's a simple explanation for all those searching, prolonged, elusive stares. In every scene it was the camera behind the other actor that held her attention. "Tell me what you think I'm into."

"I call it the other place. You know? Where you *want* to be, not where they try and tell you . . ." Something in Lora's steady yet remote gaze seemed to disconcert her. She turned her head away. "That's all."

Lora opened her purse and took out a silver cigarette case. It was empty. "Thank you so much," she said as I offered her a cigarette, then lit it. I received a stare this time, equally practiced but unseeing. "There was a period in my life—" she spoke more to the room than to either of us—"when I became interested in the spiritual side." She made it sound very distant. "It was helpful at a time I needed help, but . . ." A wreath of smoke drifted across the room. "Too many clauses in that contract, I'm afraid. I just had to break it."

"You wanted to be free," Keelie said.

She gave a flicker of irritation, like an actress who's been prompted when she really knows the line but is exploring a long pause. "I am not a finished person." She studied her feet. "Not in any sense of that word. Aren't most of us much less finished than we're led to believe? People who tell us how to live our lives always want us to make the best of what we've got. But how do they know what we've got? There can be so much *more*—"

She stood up, holding the cigarette between her fingers. She began walking slowly around the room. The movement was like taking direction in a scene; I imagined the camera following it. She opened her mouth to speak again, drew on her cigarette instead. In the middle of the room she hesitated, giving us both the same slight, measured smile. She picked up the little transistor radio and switched it on. Rock music blared out at us. Turning the selector, she picked up various stations, music, voices, crackling spaces between them. At one station she paused, listening to a voice so distorted by interference that you couldn't even be sure what language it was speaking. She turned the selector again, then moved it back. The voice had gone and there was only silence, like the silence outside. She switched it off.

"I travel with one of these myself. Often I'm in a strange place and switch it on, and I get a station for a moment, then never hear it again. The air's so full of them."

Keelie said, "Wow."

She frowned. "You never thought about that? People getting on each other's wavelengths for a moment?"

"You did it so beautifully," Keelie said, then stared at her. "I get the strangest feeling."

"Yes, I imagine you sometimes do."

"You've known about this whole thing. Since it started."

She made a small, deprecating gesture. "Is it something one can know? It's not a *fact* . . ." She returned to the couch. "Not yet, anyhow." Hands folded in her lap. "How silent you both suddenly are." Then, in a rather abrupt way, addressing the question to me: "Have you found, in this country, a cruelty about the past?"

"Yes, they're too eager to decide something is too old, out of date, useless."

She nodded. The hands clutched each other for a moment. "And pull it down or break it up or in some other way erase it from the present. But the past is beautiful as well as . . ." A little shiver passed through her body. "Really unforgivable," she said, smiled at Keelie and asked her for an ashtray. Still sitting on the floor and hugging herself, overwhelmed by the sight of Lora but not really listening to her, Keelie didn't respond at first.

"*Ashtray.*" Impatience made it sound like a demand this time. "For my cigarette, dear!"

Bringing her one, I asked where she lived now.

"I like to travel." Another direct, unperceiving glance. "I haven't bothered with a place of my own in years. Material possessions . . ." Smiling again at Keelie, she dismissed them. "I lead the gypsy life."

Keelie stiffened, as if she'd made an unexpected connection. "If you travel a lot, I'm sure I saw you on TV. On a news program. A plane had been hijacked—"

"So you caught that, did you?" Amused rather than surprised, Lora leaned toward her. "I was only on camera a moment or two. When I realized it, I moved away."

Keelie flashed me a triumphant look. "I knew it! Even though I called the airline and they said you weren't on that plane—"

"Not too fast," Lora said calmly. "I never said I was on that plane."

Keelie's face went blank. "You weren't?"

"No."

"But if I saw you . . . ?" Keelie faltered, the look in her eyes almost panic-stricken.

A ceremony followed. I couldn't imagine its purpose and it excluded me, anyway. All I knew was that Lora had decided to put Keelie to a test. Still leaning forward, face quietly attentive, hands still, she spoke in an unexpectedly hard voice, slicing words like a knife. "Work it out for yourself!"

Keelie dropped forward imploringly to her knees. She showed no surprise, only an anxiousness to please.

"What's the use of *seeing* me if you don't pay attention?" The voice kept its cutting edge. "If you don't listen?"

No answer.

"I shall be very disappointed if you can't think this little thing through."

Keelie had turned white. "Please, I need a minute!"

"You can do it quicker than that, if you try."

"Maybe it'll help if I close my eyes." Keelie did so. "But don't go away."

Still not moving, Lora waited. Outside, the silence was broken by a low purring sound. Through the window I saw, in the distance, the gardener mowing a lawn. The others didn't notice. When the trace of a smile appeared at the corners of Lora's mouth, I saw it reach Keelie's mouth a moment later, like an echo.

"Oh, I get it! You'd come in on another plane. It landed around the same time and you were just waiting to go through customs when—"

"I knew you could do it," Lora said. Her voice was soft now. "You have a perfectly good mind. It's just out of practice. If we have any talents at all, we must keep them in practice, no matter what . . ."

It was over. Opening her eyes, Keelie searched Lora's face for approval. The actress didn't look at her but consulted her watch and got alertly to her feet. "And now I'm afraid I have to go."

"Must you?"

She was already halfway across the room. "Yes, I really must."

Outside the front door, she took a deep breath of air and admired the beauty of the day. We walked on either side of her toward the open gates. The cab still waited. Below lay the city, stretching endlessly away; we saw it as from a plane coming in to land. She stopped, laying a hand on each of our arms. "My, how it's grown. When I first lived up here, it was like the beginning of the world. I woke up one morning, went onto my balcony and saw a deer drinking from my pool." Then she laughed. "How sentimental that sounds. One should never resent change. It's a shock at first, of course. But then you realize it's only a trick."

The driver held the cab door open. She seemed not to notice this, nor Keelie's desolation at the prospect of losing her. "When I was just starting to be an actress," she said, still gazing at the city below, "I went to a teacher, a remarkable man who died years ago. He explained something that became the key for whatever I was able to do." A quick glance at Keelie. "All words are lies, and anyone who speaks can't help being a liar. That's because when we find words to describe something, we turn it into something else. Speech wasn't invented in order to communicate." She shook her head, amused by the absurdity of the idea. "The intensity of the world was just too great to face in silence."

"How could you use this idea," I asked, "as an actress?"

"By not speaking. The only times I really liked myself on the screen was when I had a close-up but didn't speak. What they call a reaction shot. I think I was really rather good then. Nobody could be sure exactly what I meant, or what I was thinking. I was just myself." She turned to Keelie. "Whenever you saw me, I never spoke, did I?"

Keelie shook her head.

"But now I've been talking quite a lot. You're probably seeing someone quite different."

"No," Keelie said quietly. "You're the same."

Thoughtful, Lora's eyes rested on her for a moment.

"And you're almost . . ."

The eyes flickered. "Go on."

"It may sound ridiculous."

"Don't be shy."

"I didn't tell you that one time, in the middle of the night, when I couldn't sleep . . ." Keelie described the sight of her in the street, breathing the cold air. Then, in a wondering voice: "I've been waiting, today, for you to look like that again. And several times you've started to, but . . ."

Lora didn't answer for a moment. Her eyes remained on Keelie with the same thoughtful expression. When she spoke, she sounded completely matter-of-fact, almost breezy. "It sounds exactly like a shot we did in *Secret Wife*. We were on location right outside this house. And I remember the night was unusually cold. It turned out, somehow, to be helpful."

Keelie licked her lips, as if her mouth felt dry. "What were you thinking about in that shot?"

"This is really . . ." A look of satisfied reminiscence came over Lora's face. "I said to the director, This is very important, I don't want to do it the usual way, I don't want people to have the slightest idea what's going to happen next, in fact I want to give them the surprise of their lives."

From the way Keelie stared, I decided she must finally be recognizing that elusive look on Lora's face.

"You see, I was making up my mind to kill myself," Lora said. "And in the very next shot . . ." She glanced up the driveway, apparently dismissing the whole episode from her mind. "I must speak to the gardener before I go, there are one or two things . . . Even if a place isn't lived in, it should be kept up. I prefer places like people, always ready." With a gesture that somehow struck me as out of character, she placed an arm lightly around Keelie's waist. "Would you like to walk up there with me?"

Keelie nodded. She said to me, "I'll call you later." But I felt that I no longer existed for her. Her face was blank, like someone after a stroke. I was struck by the way that Lora smiled for a moment. She looked, I felt sure, exactly the way that Keelie had seen her in the middle of that night, outside the house. It was impossible to describe or to forget, and I even wondered whether she'd really smiled at all. They started toward the house. It seemed farther away than before. Back in his seat, the cab driver flicked the pages of a magazine.

Next evening, when Keelie still hasn't called, I give her a ring. No reply, and the same thing next day. A receptionist at the Beverly Hills Hotel informs me that Miss Chase has checked out. Naturally she leaves no forwarding address.

In the hills, the gates to the driveway stand open. I can hear a distant click of shears. A truck is parked near the house and several men are busy trimming trees. They lop off a branch and sunlight pours through the lacy opening like honey. The lodge is in shadow, Keelie's motorcycle leaning against the wall. The front door has drifted off the latch. The silence in the room where I first met Keelie said, *Everything is fine, everything is beautiful*; the silence here says, *Into thin air.* Her absence is made more final by the lack of signs of departure. It feels like entering a place that's been turned into a museum, everything just so, as

it was when somebody lived there. Days will go by now
without change. Outside, gardens will be watered and fresh
flowers planted, the house will keep up its appearance of
youth, but Keelie's lodge will only invite a little dust. Like
the dead man at the wheel of his car, and the wounded
one who hurried away down the street, the nowhereness of
Keelie is not even reported in the newspapers.

Next to the transistor radio on the table is an ashtray
containing Lora's cigarette butt, with a brilliant lipstick
stain, a tiny glaring patch of color in the room. The bedroom looks very dingy. Keelie's few clothes remain in the
closet and slung across a chair. A pair of worn sandals lies
on the floor, and a night light plugged into the wall has
been left burning. Across the bed, arms extended, is her
white bathrobe. I have no idea why I pick it up, the gesture
seems automatic, but I discover three laundry tags clipped
to the hem. One of them says DRAK, another CARS, and
another, more faintly, the first four letters of my name.

When Gary went off, this robe that he liked to wear
was in my laundry basket. It never occurred to me that
he'd taken it, in fact I later accused the laundry of having
lost it. They never found it, of course, and I bought a new
one. It's not because the terrycloth is starting to wear out,
or because Gary gave it to Keelie, or even because I don't
need it, that I don't want this robe any more. It just seems
to belong here and should not be disturbed, like the cigarette butt, the blow-ups of Che and Arlo, the silent radio.
I lay it back on the bed and the empty arms fall sideways.
I stare at them. It is my reaction shot.

EPILOGUE:
ETC.

A deep, shuddering sound wakes me this morning. Doors and windows are rattling everywhere and I start up, thinking, *Earthquake?* No, only a sonic boom. I'm not at home but lying on a couch, wearing some of my clothes. Blinds are lowered over windows. When the rattling stops, I hear a sound like bells. In the half-light I can make out a group of antique milk-glass jars, shivering against each other on a table. They stop, and there's yet another sound. The room seems alive with people breathing.

It begins to come back. Last night the front door opened to a living room filled with candlelight and people I didn't know. Then I saw Judd, who'd invited me. A succession of names, Larry, Kathy, Tom, Lennie, Barbara, Dennis, to whom I never really fitted faces. More of them in other rooms. Pop music on the phonograph, some aimless dancing, then a great deal of listening to silence. A group went for a swim in the pool, in a rather eerie subaqueous light. A tall, light-skinned Negro, offering me a hookah, declaimed sternly, *Young man, young man, your arm's too short to box with God.* Then the moon was almost down and they blew out most of the candles, joining each other on beds and couches. Laughter, moans, a few squeals of mock protest, and clothes coming off. Two people disappeared by themselves into a closet, but all the rest was open-ended.

Accustomed now to the half-light, I get up and step over someone who lies on the floor with a black sombrero covering his face. A girl in a yellow robe like a Buddhist monk's is stretched along the window seat, her mouth wide open. The Negro sleeps under the grand piano. All doors remain open, and the sound of breathing comes from everywhere; arms and limbs protrude from sleeping bodies interlaced on the beds, and the couple who went into the closet are still there, side by side, propped up like naked dummies against the wall. The kitchen is piled with unwashed glasses and dishes. From the top of the stove I excavate a kettle and fill it with water. Outside the window hang branches of a beautiful orange bougainvillea. I yawn and stare at them while waiting for the kettle to boil.

A finger gooses me sharply, a burst of laughter follows, I turn around and see Judd standing right behind me. He has wild red curly hair, a Mexican mustache, amused eyes with the skin around them faintly crinkled. Here is the fixed and final image of him: the morning after, dazed but unwaveringly cheerful in a pair of rumpled shorts.

"So what happened to *you*?"

"When?"

"After the *premier service,* in my bedroom. I didn't see you again."

"I went to sleep."

"So early?" He looks almost shocked. "Baby, it went on forever, everywhere. I've only slept a couple of hours." It was in the bushes, he tells me, and under water, and in the back of someone's vintage Cadillac.

Well, I didn't stay the course; I slept. It seems extraordinary in a way, with everyone around still screwing, but I slept rather well.

The kettle boils and Judd finds some instant coffee. We stroll out to the terrace above the pool. The morning is overcast and cool. In the dull light, purple azaleas and golden hibiscus stand out brilliantly. A few bougainvillea leaves float in the pool, as well as a girl.

"Who's that?" Judd asks.

"I don't know."

We lean back in redwood chairs, grateful for the air. Judd says, "Thank God there's no sun." He beams indiscriminately at me, the girl in the pool, the flowers, the gray sky, the hills. Then he sighs. "Better face it. I'm thirty-four and a day."

"Not a bad age."

He shakes his head. "But I really ought to . . . After all," he says absurdly, "I'm a serious person. You know that."

Judd is afflicted with charm. I'm afraid it is all he has, apart from money and dreams. The money solves a lot of problems, but the dreams create others. They start again now. How do people become actors and writers and painters?

"Talent."

He laughs. "I'm loaded with it." It's true that last year, for a few weeks, he painted, and this year he's made two TV commercials, and he told me recently over the phone that he had an idea for a movie script. "Too much is my problem."

"But you're the laziest person I know."

Agreeing, he laughs again. The twinkly look returns to his eyes. What he *will* do, he decides, starting tomorrow, is fix up that old summerhouse at the end of the garden. It should be a great place for—

"You've got more than enough places, Judd." A girl sits down beside us, wearing culottes, a sweatshirt with GO in green letters across the front, and diamond earrings. She looks at me and wonders where we've met before. I remember her from last night but I'm fairly sure that was the first time I saw her.

"No, we've met. It'll come back to me."

One of those conversations. Her name is Michele and she has an air of being socially well connected. She notices the girl floating in the pool and asks who she is, as if expecting a name from the Four Hundred.

"Well, baby," Judd says, "did you get enough to eat?"

She pats his hand. "One always does here. I can't wait for you to be thirty-five."

"I may never make it. Thirty-four feels like a pretty good age to die. Especially when people bring you such beautiful presents for your birthday." He stretches an arm along the back of each of our chairs. "I got everything I wanted."

People are waking up and coming out of the house. Some of them wear dark glasses. Larry, Kathy, Tom, Lennie, Barbara, Dennis and the others move past us along the terrace, to the driveway packed with cars. They wave casually to Judd and hope to see him again soon. He waves back and says, "A pleasure to have had you all." Then Michele gets up to go. We watch her drive off in a Jaguar, following the line of cars. They are all gone, and a silence lingers, and a feeling of emptiness comes from the house, as from a hotel at the end of the season. I start to get up, but Judd pulls me down. I suppose he doesn't want to be alone, but when I glance at his face it is utterly remote. His eyes are half closed, he passes his hand across his stomach.

A voice calls plaintively: "Hey! Anyone? Please!"

The girl has climbed out of the pool. In a dripping shirt that reaches just below her crotch, she has a waiflike air. She walks slowly toward us. She has fair hair almost down to her waist, dripping too, large blue eyes and slightly protruding, rabbity teeth. Her gums show when she smiles. Her name is Frances. Judd says that he recognizes her, she came with Dennis.

"No, I don't know anyone called Dennis."

"So who brought you?"

"Larry, I think." She looks puzzled. "But two days ago I was in Big Sur. It gets confusing. Did everyone leave?"

"Looks like it," Judd says.

"That's terrible. Someone should have waited for me. Larry, or someone."

I ask how long she's been in the water.

"I don't know. I woke up kind of early and came out to float."

Judd is watching her with the same remote expression, lids drooping over his eyes, hand still stroking his stomach. Finally he asks, "So what do you want to do?"

"I don't know. I don't have anything to do."

"Then why not hang around for a while?"

"Okay." Her voice sounds numb. Shirt and hair drip pathetically. Judd takes her by the hand and suggests she might like to change into something dry.

"Okay."

He starts to lead her into the empty house, then looks back at me over his shoulder. "I'll be checking in with you pretty soon, old friend." And then a quick, wry grimace. "Thirty-four and a day!"

I am left looking at a trail of wet footprints. A line of chairs faces the pool with orange bougainvillea leaves floating on the water. The front door, as always, remains open. Judd's voice comes from the hallway. "Is there anyone you should call, Frances? Anyone who'll be wondering where you are?"

"No. There's no one in the world."

McNally Editions reissues books that are not widely known but have stood the test of time, that remain as singular and engaging as when they were written. Available in the US wherever books are sold or by subscription from mcnallyeditions.com.